Mustang Bally

Lulu.com

First published in United States of America by the Ballymun Library Writers Group, 2019.

US ISBN: (paperback) 978-0-244-48060-8

1 3 5 7 9 10 8 6 4 2

Books printed by Lulu.com are available at special discounts for bulk purchases. For more information, please contact www.lulu.com

Printed and bound by www.lulu.com

Table of Contents

Foreword

In 2018, I was honoured to be chosen as one of UNESCO/Dublin City of Literature Writers-in-Residence, alongside Declan Burke. During the residency, I worked with different library writing groups around the city. Many of these libraries were in locations that were new to me, like Ballyfermot and Ballymun, and to receive such a warm welcome from the groups any time I visited is something I'll always be grateful for. I would get the bus back to the city centre feeling energised creatively, and lucky to have been given this opportunity.

In Ballyfermot, I was impressed by the discipline I encountered. The group had a great professionalism to it - these were motivated writers, improving and succeeding. But it was also good craic at the meetings and the ambience was light. In Ballymun, there was a palpable creative energy in the room, a sense that imagination ruled and anything at all was possible. Experiment and play were championed. These writers were studying their craft too, developing and fine-tuning their pieces and performances.

Both groups inspired me greatly during my residency. They reminded me of why I love writing, storytelling and reading. They reminded me of the kindness that fellow artists offer each other by way of listening, encouragement, and understanding. Writing, and reading, are solitary acts but in a community of like-minded people, they become a way to connect and share.

Ballyfermot and Ballymun's writers were inspirational too in that they clearly displayed two great forces of creativity – focus and flow, and now, with this dazzling anthology, they add a third – collaboration.

Read and be thrilled,

Elizabeth Reapy, April 2019

About Ballyfermot Writers' Group

Supported and facilitated by Ballyfermot library and Dublin City Council's Public Libraries Division, Ballyfermot Writers' Group was established in 2016. They meet with a ping every second Wednesday in Ballyfermot library from 6.30 p.m.

In May 2017, they were chosen to host an event, *Between the Bookcases*, which was part of the *Dublin International Literature Festival 2017* comprising songs, stories, sketches and conceptual art – on the night they sent a fictional hug to Manchester via Morrissey and Will Self. The comedian and writer, Kevin Gildea, worked with the group in preparation for this event.

The consequent Podcast, produced by Ballyfermot radio station, *Together FM*, is available to listen to at the following link -

They also produced their first anthology of writing last year to celebrate Ballyfermot's 70th birthday entitled, *The Flying Superhero Clothes Horse 2018 – Ballyer is 70!*, with contributions from Joe Duffy, Finbar Furey, Declan O'Rourke, Neville Thompson, Jimmy Murphy and Kevin Gildea. The launch of this anthology, in May, was also chosen as an event in the *Dublin International Literature Festival 2018*.

New members are always welcome. Simply contact Ballyfermot library for more information.

How it works

Unholster your pencil and write creatively on the spot to a bespoke, tinselled prompt given out on the night. Then read what you've written to the group for lavish praise, iridescent bouquets and international awards.

Or bring prepared writing along with you and read that if you wish. The choice is yours. Just turn up on the night with your own pencil!

About Ballymun Writers' Group

The Ballymun Writers group has been meeting weekly for a few years now, facilitated by the American born singer/poet/artist Nancy Owens. Every Wednesday they spend two hours working through flash fiction exercises, or beating out street poetry or tending Japanese bonsai style Haiku and Senryu. Previous members such as Sylvija Jones went on to publish well received books of their own. The group published an anthology of their work in 2018, which is available on Amazon in paperback and as an audiobook narrated by the individual authors.

"Portraits n Stuff" with Anne Marie McGrane

"Portraits n Stuff is an arts business created by Ballyfermot artist Anne Marie McGrane. Customers submit their photographs by email and have them transformed into colourful illustrated portraits, see examples at **http://www.portraitsnstuff.ie**

Living and working in Dublin, Anne Marie has studied both animation and fine art and spent over a decade working as an arts facilitator and teacher, both in the formal education sector and in community education.

Anne Marie's art style bridges the gap between fine art and illustration. Heavily influenced by printing techniques, her finished artworks have the bold line and texture of woodblock prints. However, they are finished off delicately with watercolour and pencil as a fine art portrait would be."

Looking Down
By A.J. Bennett

She scans the pavement, head down, looking for threats. A tree root thrusts the tarmac up to meet the wheels of her rollator. She toddles along, studiously avoiding lifted pavement slabs, a slalom for seniors. Cars too big jut out of driveways too small to add to the hazards. A walk is no longer a carefree commune with nature and neighbours. It's a study in obstacle avoidance, its threats to life and limb. I must not fall, I must not fall, I must not fall, the refrain running through her head. Rain-slicked sidewalks are her enemy, wet leaves on the footpath are her enemy, frosty winter pavements are her enemy. A yappy little dog threatens, dancing and barking behind her, nipping at her heels. She shouts at the owner. She dare not turn and lose her balance lest she fall, fall, fall. Empty reassurances from the owner - he won't bite you! How could he possibly know how it feels to be frail and afraid. He'll get his turn.

Ann Herkes

I would really like to thank my Mum for saying to me, "just do it", it gave me courage to try.

I would really like to thank all those who have held my hand on this journey and especially Peter O'Sullivan who listened to me saying over and over "dae yi get it?" He got it, he heard me, seen me and validated me as a poet. Thank You All xo.

Ambivalence
By Ann Herkes

Ambivalence is an internal pull
of opposite poles.
An eternally stretched
Elastic band.
A struggle to know
just what
to do
Right or
left
Right or
wrong
A mental torment
a state of despair
A sense of being torn
ripped in two
indecisive
left confused
ambivalent
not knowing it
unsure
scared
to choose
Ambivalence
the huge unknown
rocks my
foundation
shakes me
to the core.
leaves me
apprehensive
never
sure.

Little Thoughts
By Ann Herkes

Little thoughts
Gather
Momentum
And Giant
Dreams are
Unleashed
Spurring
Me
On
To
Know
There
Is
More
To
Me.
Giving me
Courage
To
Step up
And
Dare
To
Believe
That
A
Poet
I
Can
Be
Giving

Me
Confidence
To
Stand
Up
Here
For
All
To
See
Exposing
My
Thoughts
And
Feelings
My
Fears
My
Terror
My
Shame at
No being literate enough
Laying
Out
Vulnerable sides
That would have me
Run and hide
Scared you
May
Slate
Me.
Little thoughts
Gather
Huge

Strengths
Over
The
Years
As they are
Exposed
As
Protectors
Of the
Status
Quo
And
I
Have
Outgrown
The
Need
To
Stay
Low.
Little
Thoughts
Have
Grown
Into
Every
Day
Actions
That
Are
Easy
To
Step
Up

To
And
Do.
Little
Thoughts
Have
Huge
Outcomes
Changing
Life's
Direction
When one
Dares to step
Into new
Shoes.

Sugar Fixes
By Ann Herkes

I feel like Puking up
Cause I just ate nonstop
Chocolate here
Crisps there
Poisoning
My
System
With
TOXIC
CRAP
that's
Advertised
As
Connection
With
Other's
By
Having
A BREAK
Á cuppa
A biscuit
Or
Two.
But one's
Not
Enough
Not
When
I
eat
that

STUFF
IT
TRIGGERS
ME OFF
FOR ANOTHER
AIN
ANOTHER
CAUSE
ONE just
AINT
ENOUGH
TO SATISFY
THE
HUNGRY
TIGER
WHO ROARS
FOR MORE
AND TERRIFIES
ME.
Making
Me
Small
and
Tiny
A
Little
Weak
Figure
who's
Failed again
And
Swallowed
Her
Trigger.

Sugar
Fixes
Don't
Fix
Anything
Don't
Stop
The ache
The
Sadness
The
Emptiness
Sugar
Is
A
Trick
My
Mind
Uses
To
Avoid.
Feeling
ain
the
Vast aching
Void
of
<u>Aloneness</u>

This is a journey
By Ann Herkes

This is a journey
of
Endings
ain
Beginnings
Without Letting Go
the New
cannae exist
without Letting go
I leave myself
Stuck in limbo
in that
Tragic place
of
"What if".
Stuck between
Fantasy
ain
Reality
Scared
Shiteless
of
Giving
Scared
Shiteless
of
Receiving
Scared
Shiteless
of
Breathing
In

Life
Breathing
In
Experience
Breathing
In
Fright
Ain the delight
Of
Overcoming it.
Breathing in
Loss
Ain
All
the pure painful Grief that Stings
Without feelings those feelings
Ain
Letting Go
I
cannae step into the New
Ain aw that will bring.
Without Letting Go
I will be paralysed
Stuck
In
Time
Wasting
Time
As
Time
Is
All
I've
Got.

Anne Dunphy took early retirement from the Civil Service three years ago. And never looked back! Her motto in life is "Carpe Diem" i.e. Seize The Day (a Latin phrase used by the Roman Poet Horace)

"We are here for a very short time, we are basically just passing through, therefore it is up to each one of us to enjoy life, live life to the fullest, be mindful and have no regrets."

The City That Never Sleeps
By Anne Dunphy

For as long as I can remember I always dreamed of going to this place, New York City and now we had arrived. We had taken the plane from my home town Dublin and landed at the infamous airport, JFK. A sharp intake of breath and I was finally "here"! We didn't have long to wait as we flagged down a taxi and arrived in a beautiful neon-lit Times Square.

"Times Square", a scene from times past where a naval officer took his sweetheart in his arms and kissed her in front of a throng of people as they celebrated the end of World War II. A place that boasts one of the tallest Christmas trees in the world and where people gather together to happily engage in the countdown to New Year's Day, it just breathed a sense of excitement to me. I couldn't help but smile!

I remember when we got out of our taxi, the view was just spectacular. There were many skyscrapers; so many bright lights, the infamous "yellow cabs" that appear in so many American movies over the years and here we were actually getting out of one and seeing others pass by oblivious to our excitement! We saw so many people toing and froing, so focused and going about their daily business!

Tantalizing aromas emanating from the busy restaurants that were lining the street. Everything about this iconic place was big, big, BIG! I now understood why they affectionately called New York City, "The Big Apple". Never in all my years did I ever see such a place, so distracted by it all and my excitement, I looked upwards and all around and simply just took it all in. My emotions became a sponge, a mop, I dare not wring it out, I wanted to just bottle it all up and savour the moment!

I thought to myself "Me thinks I am in Heaven!". I thought to myself "It's all and more" than what I expected. New York City certainly was not disappointing me. We were after all on a holiday of a lifetime and for the ten glorious days we were going to be here, we were going to maximize our time and create incredible memories that would last an eternity for us both to absorb and remember.

New York City was a destination high on my "bucket list", I knew that the moment my heels touched down on the tarmac of this iconic city, I would be savouring every single moment. I brought my Kodachrome with me, fully charged and ready so that I could document each passing moment and day and relish looking back on all my beautiful photos of our trip to "The Big Apple"

As one could imagine, day one of our trip to New York was met with excitement and it wasn't long before the evening came to a close and we retired for the evening and rested our happy but weary bones knowing that when the sun set the next day, we would be waking up in an incredible vibrant city with many things to do that we wanted! Our schedule was packed to the gills! Eyes heavy, bones weary, heads on soft pillows, our first day over.

The following morning we woke early to the familiar sounds that were consistent with living in a busy town and had a beautiful breakfast. I remember it clearly. We delighted in enjoying a beautiful fruity yoghurt that we had purchased the night before in one of the supermarkets. It was quite a healthy breakfast if I remember clearly, fresh fruit and yoghurt and not a pancake with maple syrup or butter in sight! It was a fruity feast of the juiciest apples, cantaloupe, grapes, apricots, bananas, plums and the sweetest cherries.

I swiped the napkin from my lips and felt as satisfied as I could, breakfast couldn't have been more perfect and now we were on a mission! A day of cycling awaited us. Fully attired and looking very athletic, our destination was the town of Midtown Manhattan and we had to take the subway! I was so excited by that! We boarded the train fully attired in our cycling gear and taking the subway, it dawned on me that we had almost naturalized ourselves as Americans if it wasn't for our giveaway Irish accent, we might have pulled it off! We headed to the bike hire shop and was met by a very happy-go-lucky chap, I remember he was very smiley and had a happy disposition. After a short chat with him, we were all set to go and discover Manhattan; we had our bicycles, we had our helmets and most of all, our wits about us!

We cycled the streets of Broadway and wide busy roads. I could hear the sounds of the anxious traffic, the tooting car horns bellowed different tones. We cycled through East Central Park and along The Hudson Greenway. We saw so many people roller-blading, joggers, walkers and fellow cyclists, it was just a hub of energy!

The Hudson River was a picture of calm and I was reminded of the time a brave pilot landed his troubled plane upon the waters and saved the entire crew and passengers; this was where it happened, my imagination was destined to run riot but it remained as calm as the waters that day. The sun was shining and arching over the city was the most beautiful rainbow one ever did see. An eclectic array of colours, such a colourful rainbow.

We cycled over the infamous Brooklyn Bridge arriving at Coney Island. My first thoughts were that I had never seen a place like it before, it was pure Nirvana. Blazing sunshine rippled through, golden sand sparkled when the sun shone upon it; it was dazzling, such an idyllic place. I watched from afar as children built sandcastles, their parents relaxing nearby with a glass of chilled wine in their hands. There was a great sense of peace.

As our first evening exploring New York came to a close, we headed home after what we felt was a most delightful day full of fun and adventure and feeling energized, liberated! My partner and I were looking forward to the rest of the holiday. We both agreed that cycling was one of the best ways of exploring New York City.

In the days that followed, we cycled over Washington Bridge and cycled to New Jersey which I personally thought was so beautiful, such a contract to the hustle and bustle of The Big Apple; New Jersey was beckoning more rural lands.

The quiet country roads, the countryside, the farmlands, the birds that sang whilst perched on wooden fences to the birds that flew past us as we cycled! The normality of it all, the familiar sounds of a dog barking and cockerels crowing interrupted the feathery chorus that we were enjoying but we didn't mind too much, it didn't seem to disturb what we felt was a most tranquil place to be. We knew we had clocked up so many miles on our bicycles that it didn't seem so important as the places we were seeing.

In the final days of our trip of a lifetime, we visited the iconic Chrysler Building, The United Nations building. We climbed the Empire State Building where once an enormous gorilla from the Roaring '20s clung to it for dear life and delighted many that watched him on the silver screen; we could see for miles, such a fantastic view!

We cycled to Orchard Beach in The Bronx and brought our faithful bikes on the ferry to Staten Island. I remember the sailing was calm, the sky a deep cobalt blue, it was the perfect setting for taking photographs of the infamous Statue of Liberty that presided over the great city of New York like a goddess; there she stood alone in the harbour and yet she wasn't really alone; she was always surrounded by at least "somebody".

We cycled through Flushing Meadow to the infamous Arthur Ashe Stadium and I was delighted in seeing my tennis hero Roger Federer triumph as winner of his match!

To encapsulate, I really think The Big Apple is "one hell" of a great place! To me, there's no place like it. A City that never sleeps, true to a song penned so many years ago, "so good they named it twice", New York, New York ...

Our bicycles now rested ... our memories of a great visit forever in our minds, through the medium of pictures we can see and in our dreams when we revisit..

Life Is For Living
By Anne Dunphy

Life is short, so make the most of it, take enjoyment out of what you do
bit by bit.
Do the things you love, this will help you evolve.
Go for a walk, listen to music, phone a friend, catch up and talk.
Enjoy nature, say a prayer, savour a meal, life's simple pleasures.
Not a big deal, but if sad, will certainly heal.

Don't take partners, spouses, friends or family for granted.
Express, let them know how much you care.
Life is short, life is for living
Remember this, be aware.

Simple things in life are free.
Cycling, Gardening, Walking Reading,
a few hobbies to mention
past times I enjoy without apprehension.

Try not to worry, don't sweat the small stuff,
words which are not off the cuff,
embrace life and it's challenges
always find the balance.
Find time for reflection.
Don't look back, be mindful,
the future will be a revelation.

Do good for others, some small act
show people you are true, thus guaranteed an impact,
be loyal, don't offend, be positive
this should be our main prerogative.

In conclusion, be healthy, eat well
don't ruminate or dwell.
Keep thoughts positive, look after your mind,
this needs to be outlined.

Enjoy holidays at home or abroad, laugh, sing, applaud.
Seek fulfilment in life, make this rife!!
We are only passing through,
ultimately it's up to me and you,
do good by giving, life is short, life is for living
therefore, I believe these words are fitting!!

Mother
By Anne Dunphy

I was so lucky to have a fantastic Mother,
she really and truly was like no other.
She worked so hard at home,
she cooked, washed, cleaned, shopped and worked herself to the bone.
I remember as a child, she was always in the house.
When we came home from school our dinner was always on the table
and one later for her spouse.

My Mother idolised each one of us,
this info I impart on thus.
She didn't drink except at Christmastime,
she would have the odd advocaat or babycham,
then again she wouldn't bother and just opt for a lemon and lime.

My mam loved her auld cigarettes,
if she didn't have one she would fret
the brand that she smoked was Players Mild,
this I remember as a child.
My mam absolutely loved her garden,
she adored flowers and vegetables into the bargain
she led a very simple life,
I know for sure she was a terrific wife.
My mother was kind, selfless, loving and true,
a gem, one in a million and great craic too.

I for one will always remember the 28th May 1989
I wish I could say it was an ordinary day and everything was fine
Alas it wasn't, it was the day my lovely mother departed the universe
I was heartbroken, as were all of us
A few days later we saw the Undertakers,
so they could organise the hearse.

It's still hard to believe my beautiful mother is deceased thirty years
For me, I will never forget her, my angel.
I know she's happy now, so no need for tears.
Love you Mam!!

Betsy
By Anne Dunphy

Oh how I love my bike, I've travelled to Howth, Malahide,
Leixlip, Dunlaoghaire and Bray,
My partner and myself adore these trips and we very rarely go astray.
We have cycled in Carlow, Sligo, Leitrim, Waterford, Belfast and Cork
My favourite spot by far has to be New York.
I recall Queens, The Bronx, Staten Island, Harlem, New Jersey
and Manhattan, oh what memories, places which never go out of
fashion.
My bike, my love has transported me to many a city, Amsterdam,
The Hague, Rotterdam, Brussels, Oporto, The Camino and more.
I have donned protective gear so not to become saddle sore.
Cycling is a big part of my life, nothing is better for releasing strife.
Cycling has so many health benefits, it's proven to be a big hit.
It's great for strengthening bones, for weight loss for shifting the
pounds.
Cycling decreases stress, Wow aren't we blessed.
Cycling is free, excellent for the heart, It's never too late to start.
Life for me would not be the same without my bike
On our travels, we have encountered many a hike.
True enough I had a few falls, now this I do recall.
I recovered to tell the tale, Betsy my bike never fails.
I will conclude by saying you are a gem,
cycling a leisure pursuit one can't condemn.
United we'll continue our cycling travels,
I look forward in anticipation to see what unravels.

Mickey Murrays
By Brendan Shanahan

Mickey Murrays was a stream that meandered between the banks of the Royal Canal and the walls of Mountjoy Prison. In summertime, we used to make our way to the stream and catch pinkeens.

Mickey Murrays was famous for more than pinkeens. There was a series of jumps. The jumps at the lower end of the stream were easier than those further up as the distance between the banks widened and became steeper. The last and most difficult jump was the Abbot jump, not because of any particular religious or monastic significance, but because the first person to jump it was called Abbot. The Abbot jump had a badge of honour attached to it and all other jumps had to be completed first before attempting it.

Wardick was the first of our group to attempt the Abbot jump. He jumped and landed heavily but safely. He shouted across that it was easy. My turn eventually came. There was plenty of advice, like jump as high up as you can, bend your legs, keep your feet together and avoid the protruding rock on the landing side. With all that advice around, I guess I must have been the last to jump. I considered my options and there were none. I launched myself into the air. There was a sense of exhilaration but no outer world experience. It was over in a flash and time to move on.

Unlike Abbot, I have never been first at anything in my life. However, I am not aware of anyone who jumped the Abbot jump after me. On that basis, I am claiming to be the last person to make the jump. The Abbot jump has disappeared along with Mickey Murrays and I think that I am safe in making this claim.

Happy Days
By Brendan Shanahan

"Mr Byrne" we have the results. The telephone rang. The Consultant apologised and excused herself to take the call. She left the room.

He knew what it would be like in a nursing home. Could he stand the smell? Could he take it when he would not be allowed out through the door? Women do better than men in these situations. Women are more flexible, more resourceful and usually have a better social network. Men are more individualistic, less resourceful and generally more stupid. Most men think that they are in charge, whereas in fact, they are not.

Brian was a musician and played extensively in nursing homes. He was a witness to the magic of music. He saw people coming alive. "South of the Border" and "It's a Long Way to Tipperary" were two of the most popular songs. "Have You Ever Been Lonely" was also perversely popular. Sean, a resident, sings "It's a long way to the Pawnshop" to the air of "It's a long way to Tipperary". His blue eyes light up when he sings. Other residents join in and the afternoon passes with sounds of laughter.

Pepe is a street dog from Chile living in Dublin. He walks in the park with Brian. Pepe has a bad hip which makes him skip from time to time. They walk together regularly and always return home safely.

"We're in the boat that we hope will float; Let the waves take us in".

Brian's latest song is about immigrants coming to Europe. "This has to go up on Facebook" he tells himself. "How do I do that"? Social media is the way forward. Pepe waddles along beside him.

Brian returns to his musings.

"Soar to the left, soar to the right. Soar to the East, soar to the West.

You can have my body, but you can't have my soul, you can have my body but my soul is my own, ok?"

A song about the superpowers ruling the world.

and

"If you'll be my rat tat too, I will send my love to you.

If you say you love me too, you'll be my rat tat too".

The only song he ever wrote as a result of a dream.

and

"Walking through the Green one morning, on a summer's day.

The dawning morning, people yawning, walking on their way.

Swans stretching out their wings and cleaning out their bills.

The park attendant, he's intending, cleaning up the thrill of the night."

This was one of his earlier songs and he always liked the imagery and storyline.

Brian's eyes shone. Pepe barks and he is drawn back to reality. Pepe is decidedly anti social and has a particular dislike of cats. In fact, he dislikes everyone most of the time. He is black, slightly overweight and a slow walker with the odd hop thrown in for good measure as a result of his dodgy hip. Despite the hip, he is very fast when it comes to chasing cats.

Brian muses again about his creations. Where do they come from? Once created; no longer his. They stand alone, god like, for better or worse. He was no Bob Dylan, but then Dylan was no Brian Byrne.

He had decided to get medical advice as his memory was not as good as it used to be. Names of people slipped away from time to time and the concentration levels not as good as they used to be. He had taken up snooker again. Shots formerly easy were now difficult. Long shots in particular posed a problem. He began to question himself and his self-confidence was shaken. After all, he didn't want to spend all his money without remembering where he spent it! He had only been married once and didn't want to wake up with somebody else and not know who she was, or where she had come from. "Time to get checked out," he thought.

At the consultation, he had gone through a battery of questions like Name, Date of Birth, Middle Name and his Mother's name. What day of the week was it and what year was it. All straight forward stuff and then a number of more difficult questions like his phone number and his wife's date of birth. He was put lying down and transported into a tunnel where his brain was photographed. Some blood tests followed.

Today was the callback visit to the Consultant for the results.

The consultant returned to the room. "Mr Byrne, is your wife with you today?" Brian did not like the sound of that. "She's not here". "Oh I thought that she would be here. I thought I saw her earlier. Will she be long?"

"She has gone shopping. She says that there is nothing wrong with me and she is gone to pick up a few things at the supermarket".

The consultant nodded knowingly. "Does your wife know everything Mr Byrne? Is she medically qualified by any chance"?

"Yes, she maintains that she knows everything. As such, she'd be wasting everybody's time studying. She has saved me a fortune over the years!".

"Everything has a place and everything should be in its place" purred the Consultant.

"Indeed you're a wise lady, it's no wonder you're a Consultant. Did you find my brain?"

"Would you prefer to wait and discuss things when your wife is present?"

"Not at all, she will be back in a while and I will explain everything to her, even though she knows everything."

"I find that wives sometimes feel excluded if their husband's health is being discussed in their absence; they tend to become angry," said the Consultant.

"You're right there" said Brian. "Now, what's the story? Get on with it."

"We have run extensive tests. I can say that there is no evidence of any major deterioration in your brain functions. Your memory has declined a little and accordingly I am recommending some memory exercises to improve matters. The internet contains some interesting applications which you can download. My secretary will give you the details. Finally, I think that you should learn to play bridge and maybe learn a foreign language. These types of activities are good for the brain."

His wife returned to the medical centre where she found him in the waiting area. "Well, what did she say?"

He replied

"Who are you? Do I know you from somewhere? Are you my treasure snatched from the bottom of the rainbow? Did you bring a crock of gold by any chance?"

"None of your guff" said his wife. "She obviously told you that there was nothing wrong. See I told you that there was nothing wrong. Come on let's go".

Later that afternoon, Brian took Pepe for a walk in the park. They both skipped in unison as he also needed a new hip. "We men will stick together" he said to Pepe. He smiled at his life as he looked forward to his next birthday on the 29 February. "Celebrate a birthday every four years. That's the way to slow things down". Pepe suddenly barked and wrenched free from the lead in pursuit of a cat. The cat scurried up an apple tree and left Pepe stranded below barking. An apple fell from the tree and hit him on the head. Eureka, he then knew that the cat would survive and that he was wasting his time, on this occasion.

Brian and Pepe returned home safely

The Politician
By Brendan Shanahan

Stroker was a fairly new politician on the way up the political ladder. He was in good form but a little apprehensive as he strode along the corridors of power. It was not often one got to see the Taoiseach privately. He did not want to pitch his hopes too high, but things on the whole were going well. His auditory assault (AA) on the Spanish Embassy had been a total success. His ploy of arranging an automatic call up every few minutes to the Embassy with a recording of his song "Ban the Gringos" blaring down the line was working well. Their telephone system had been thrown into utter disarray. The latest information to hand was that the Embassy was refusing to pay their telephone bills. He chuckled to himself. His record "Ban the Gringos" was rapidly climbing the charts, and he had plans to appear on a local radio station.

He wondered what was in the offing, perhaps a Ministry although a Junior position would be acceptable for the present. He had rehearsed this meeting in his mind on many occasions and wondered why it had taken so long. He figured the best approach would be to adopt a sombre statesmanlike attitude and to feign surprise at whatever promotion was offered.

He knocked, heard a grunt and made his entrance. The Taoiseach was busy writing on a note pad and took no notice of Stroker. Stroker took a mental note of this, a condescending ploy to be used when he would have assumed the highest mantle, in the interest of the country of course. The Taoiseach looked up and glowered across the table.

"What sort of a gobshite are you?" he enquired. "There are enough idiots in the country without having fools like you in the party."

What's up with this megalomaniac, thought Stroker who saw his political career taking a nosedive. Remember your military training in the Wicklow hills, an inner voice whispered. Diversionary tactics were required before he got to the bottom line:

"Depart from me you cursed."

Like hell I will, he thought. Stroker jumped up from his chair and with great agility leaped high into the air; hands outstretched, and began reciting from Alfred Lord Tennyson:

"He stepping down by zig zag paths and juts of pointed rock,
    Came on the shining levels of the lake"

Onomatopoeia! He hollered. The Taoiseach was dumbfounded; the plan was working. Stroker then grabbed a writing pad from the desk and while launching into rhyming couplets, scribbled the word 'Recording being made!' and tossed it back on the table. The Taoiseach being razor sharp immediately inferred that there was a breach of security and that the conversation was being bugged. He too leaped into the air shouting something about neutrality and the Brits. He then bounded up onto his mahogany table and croaked in frog-like monotones the memorable lines -

"I'm a little teapot short and stout,
    here's my handle here's my spout.
When the tea is ready hear me shout,
    lift me up and pour me out."

Just then the Taoiseach's private secretary arrived on the scene and enquired if everything was in order. This startled the Taoiseach who pirouetted sharply, too sharply as it turned out. Perhaps it was the shiny table surface that accelerated the spin, but down he went bringing with him his personal computer, which exploded, on impact with the ground. Alarm bells sounded around the building and armed detectives, guns drawn burst into the office. The private secretary was told to "spread them" by one detective who was carrying an Uzi machine gun. This detective was anxious to redeem himself following on a skirmish which he had led against a group of students queuing for a bus in Westmoreland Street. The detective had considered the gathering suspicious because of all the babbling noises coming from the queue. The battle had been sharp and swift with the students who resorted to sharpened rulers and pencil cases as a means of defence. The students' were accommodated in a local Garda station for a few days. A major diplomatic incident ensued with Spain threatening to invade Ireland unless their citizens were released. It transpired that the students were mostly Spanish.

Meanwhile back at the Taoiseach's Department, the local army unit, interrupting their game of snooker, charged headlong into the fray. Orders rang out in the mother tongue so as to confuse the enemy. The detective with the Uzi, who was of English descent, mistook the intruders for Russians who had learned the mother tongue as part of their plan to kidnap the Taoiseach or worse still, assassinate him. Their accent did not sound native to his educated ear. He immediately opened fire. His first burst peppered the walls and blew the nose off a Jack B. Yeats painting which the State had purchased for 20 million pounds. A priceless piece of art became a worthless piece of junk in nano seconds. The detective dived across the Taoiseach's body to protect him. The Taoiseach, who was now in a catatonic state and babbling incoherently in a loud voice "mutatis mutandis". Being a student of language, the detective became confused and with his brilliant mind figured that the real Taoiseach could speak only English or Irish and therefore he must be an impostor! He decided to look out for himself and managed to curl up under a heavy wooden desk. Lucky he did as the anti personnel device tossed into the room to quell the coup d'etat blew the windows out and sent a chandelier made of Waterford crystal crashing to the floor.

Meanwhile Jake and Jessica from Wyoming USA were strolling down Merrion Street and came upon the commotion. Out came the camera in time to witness the exploding windows. Out came the cops from the paddy wagon. A Garda, just posted from a Gaeltacht area pounced on the American. "Cad é sin?" He hollered pointing at the camera. Jake was startled, "What goddam city am I in? Do the natives speak American around here? Be calm, said Jessica, these foreigners are harmless and don't abuse the fairer sex". He was arrested and only managed to prove that he was not a spy on examination of the recording from his camera showing clips of his dogs – a Rottweiler and a Poodle, followed by a funeral of the Poodle, the Poodle's headstone and then a shot of the windows being blown out of Government Buildings.

As for Jessica, she eloped with a sheep farmer from Kerry and has since learnt Irish. The Taoiseach is still in a mental institution and is convinced that Hitler is his father. Stroker is now a full cabinet Minister. Jake has become a fan of the Yorkshire Ripper and was last seen prowling the hills of Kerry and its environs looking for some dame called Jessica.

Camillus John was bored and braised in Dublin. He has had writing published in *The Stinging Fly, RTÉ Ten, The Lonely Crowd* and other such organs.

You may know him from such fiction as *The Woman Who Shagged Christmas, The Rise and Fall of Cinderella's Left Testicle* and, *Throwing A Sausage Back and Forth for Five Minutes Without Letting it Drop,* all of which are included in his fictionbook, *Groin Frosties With Jazzy Hand – The Pervert's Guide To Modern Fiction* (Ballyer Press 2018).

Ballyer Press also published his poembook, *Why the Privileged Need To Read Literature* in 2018 and his novel, *How To Be A Bicycle - From the Campaign for the Legalisation of Drugs in the Workplace for all Hard-Working Families* in 2019.

The Steam of My Piss is his second poembook and will be published by Ballyer Press in 2019.

Along with Declan Geraghty, he is one of the founder members of Ballyfermot Writing Group's *The Flying Superhero Clothes Horse*, Europe's premier centre for conceptual art and post-punk modernism.

He would also like to mention that Pats won the FAI cup in 2014 after 53 miserable years of not winning it.

Bus Stop Madonnas
By Camillus John

My nine year old niece is at the bus stop
outside St James' hospital.
She's with her mother.

They are playing the game,
Guess which Madonna song
this dance is from.
The sun shines.
The wind blows.
And the bus takes ages to come.
The bloody number 40 is always late
or doesn't even turn up half the time.
But no one notices.

"Is that dance *Holiday*?" "No."
"Is it *Into The Groove*?" "No."
"Is it *Vogue*?" "No."
"Is it *Material Girl*?" "No. Ma. No."
"Is it *True Blue*?"
"Yes. Three points.
Now it's your turn.
Do a Madonna dance –
hurry up Ma. Come on.
Before the bus comes."

Cookie On Capel Street 2018
By Camillus John

I remember when I was nine
and my granda brought me
into town to buy me toys
in Smyths off Henry Street.

Or he'd take me to the cinema
on Parnell Street.

Or to McDonald's
on O'Connell Street.

But especially I remember
the way he'd always stop,
on the way back to getting
the bus home,
to buy me a cookie
in a shop on Capel Street.

Elvis is Alive!
By Camillus John

I lie in bed at five in the morning and listen to the
dawn chorus through the open bedroom window.
I've thrown the blankets off
because I sweat and sweat and sweat.

It's 10 o'clock already
11 o'clock, and
I've listened to the estate
getting up and about
on a Saturday
like air pumping up a bouncy castle.

The pigeons are cooing in next
door's pigeon loft.
A motorbike's engine is being
revved and worked on in my
other neighbour's concrete shed,
and Elvis the dog from five or six
doors down the road
howls the blues along with
the ice-cream van that's screaming
The Sailor's Hornpipe
out the flake of its
cornet loudspeaker.

Elvis sings from his back garden
every single time the ice-cream van
comes around. With a gorgeous
quiver in his voice.

The van stops at the crossroads
up the street, and with a screech of brakes
and a trample of young feet;
the music stops
and Elvis -
has left the garden.

Except You Skank*
By Camillus John

(To the image of Lee 'Scratch' Perry
walking backwards along the boardwalks of life).

I was skankin'
She was skankin'
He was skankin'
They were skankin'
Brothers were skankin'
Sisters were skankin'
The priest with red trousers
was skankin'.

The man was skankin'
The woman was skankin'
Even Cinderella's left testicle
was skankin'.
The sun was skankin'
The moon was skankin'
The skankin' was skankin'
and skankin' and skankin' -

except you.

*Skank is used in the positive, reggae context of the word.

Guess Who's Coming to Dinner?
By Camillus John

Donald Trump is coming
lock up your sons and daughters.
Donald Trump is coming
watch your spoons and saucers.
Donald Trump is coming,
so keep sketch.

He's coming in an aeroplane
he suffers bad with arse pain.
He's coming in an aeroplane
he suffers bad with arse pain.
He's coming in an aeroplane,
so keep sketch.

He's coming yes he coming
because Bernie has him running.
A coward bumbox humming,
'cause he fled from Vietnam.

Ireland likes bumfluff
let's dick-kick Ireland o.
Ireland likes bumfluff
let's bitch-slap Ireland o.
Oh Ireland likes licking arse
(American arse),
so keep sketch.

He sometimes wears a sports bra
or so says his ma.
He sometimes wears a sport bra
or so says his ma.

He sometimes wears a sports bra,
so keep sketch.

He's coming yes he coming
because Bernie has him running.
A coward bumbox humming,
'cause he fled from Vietnam.

Donald Trump is coming
lock up your sons and daughters.
Donald Trump is coming
watch your spoons and saucers.
Donald Trump is coming,
so keep sketch.

How to Solve the Housing Crisis in 20 Seconds Flat with a Francis Bacon Pope's Head

By Camillus John

Imagine his head.
Imagine his head.

Ballyfermot was a big, phat, smiley
70 years of age in 2018
with a tinselled cherry on top.
The Council built all the houses
there themselves.
With no middle man.
When people were starving.

Now close your eyes.
Everyone please -
close your eyes.

(Finger click).

Picture the Minister
of Housing's head.
As I write, the current Minister
is Eoghan Murphy,
a Francis Bacon Pope's head
of a Minister of Housing,
but it might be someone else
by the time you read this.

Imagine his head.
Imagine his head.

Keep your eyes closed and

start counting to twenty.

Imagine his head.
Imagine his head.

Now picture
that head exploding into millions
and billions and zillions of pieces.
And picture each of these fragments of blood, skin, bone,
eyeball and brain
as they
turn into houses,
turn into homes,
turn into communities.

Imagine each and every
one of these new houses landing on their foundation plots
in a place of your choosing
and creating another Ballyfermot
and another Ballyfermot and
yet another Ballyfermot
to infinity and beyond.

Imagine his head.
Imagine his head.

Congrats. You've managed to solve
the housing crisis in
twenty seconds flat.
Or at least you've made a better stab
however imaginary
at solving the housing crisis
than any of the solutions
currently available

in the unexploded
Francis Bacon
Pope's head
of the current
Minister
of Housing.

Imagine his head.
Imagine his head.
(Finger click).
Now open your eyes.

The Best Kisser In Ballyer
By Camillus John

Me Da said Jimmy was a fabulous kisser.
A1. Top notch.
He and all the lads agreed.
They had proof.

Da is in James' hospital and earlier
today he was walking up and down
the corridor for exercise
when he heard a twisted yet
familiar voice coming from behind.
"Ozo! It's yourself, I don't believe it –
Ozo! Ozo! Ozo!"

Da turned and wasn't it Jimmy himself.
He hadn't seen him since a few years after school
– over fifty years ago.
And Jimmy still recognised him.
They used to go to the Ritz together
of a Saturday.

Da said one night he and
the lads were standing at the end
of the laneway on Thomond Road,
smoking,
after the dance, after getting chips
on the way home.

They heard Jimmy with his
mot canoodling,
in the porch outside her house,
a few doors up from

their current spot in the laneway.

Jimmy's mot, Noeleen,
let out a squeal –
"Jimmy, you're a great kisser you are!
Bionic."

Jimmy grabbed his chance
by the balls and
shouted up at me Da and the lads –
"Did yiz hear that, eh?
She says I'm a great kisser. I told yiz –
Didn't I? Well, didn't I?'

And me Da said Jimmy was right.
He did tell them that alright.
The bastard. He was a great kisser,
Jimmy was. The best kisser in
Ballyer. Dickhead.

The Flying Superhero Clothes Horse Himself
By Camillus John

Charlene, the chocolate-pencil
poet of Landen Road,
bent down,
to polish her shoes
until they were
switched-on-lightbulbs.
She had an interview
of squeaky-bum significance
in less than five minutes.

But as she did so
her trousers ripped
right up the arse.
"Janey Macken Street!"
she said, "This is
the Titanic of
wardrobe malfunctions.
I'm sunk now for sure –
I'll never get the job!"

There was only one individual to call,
Howie, the horse from Ballyfermot,
The Flying Superhero Clothes horse
himself.

"I'll be there in a bionic flash, Charlene,"
said Howie down the phone.
So he put his bent out of shape
clothes-hanger on his head,
packed up his lunch and
flew off the roof of The Gala

red cape fluttering
towards Charlene forthwith,
five, four, three, two minutes
before her squeaky-bum interview.

With needle, thread and thimble
Howie sewed up the ripped arse
of Charlene's trousers
like a Grand Wizard of
fashion and design.

Charlene thus strode in and knocked
them all bandy and pop-eyed
with her
written-in-milk-chocolate-pencil
poetry of the sublime;
she got the job.

Another call came in for Howie.
It was Peter, The Pyjama Girl,
from Cremona.
He'd gotten his knickers in a twist
and couldn't leave the house
for falling down.

"Don't worry Peter, I'll be there
in two shakes of a yellow tambourine,
to untwist them," said Howie,
"Thou shalt go to the ball!"

It was a glitterball to celebrate
Ballyfermot's 70th
and Peter didn't want to miss it
for he'd already got her hair

and nails done especially.

Charlene saluted Howie and
crossed-her-heart-and-hoped-to-die promised to
visit his Fiver Shop on the
California Hills soon,
very soon indeed,
if not even sooner,
to purchase some of his
horsetrepreneurial products
for his new range was now in stock.

She watched his tail and arse
as he flew up and over the
roof of the Gala, the old cinema,
towards Peter's house
where he'd gotten his
knickers into such a god-awful twist.

A Flying Superhero Clothes Horse's
work, is never done.
Ever.

They All Said This
By Camillus John

Gertrude Stein wrote about food and said this
Italo Calvino wrote about the moon and said this
John Berger wrote about seeing and said this
James Joyce wrote about wanking and said this

William Burroughs wrote about heroin and said this
William Yeats wrote eugenics and said this
Zadie Smith wrote about accents and said this
David Forster Wallace wrote about depression and said this

Vladimir Nabokov wrote about paedophilia and said this
Virginia Wolfe wrote about a room and said this
Samuel Beckett wrote about maggots and said this
Mary Shelley wrote about monsters and said this

Franz Kafka wrote about cockroaches and said this
Jane Austin wrote about hierarchy and said this
Allen Ginsberg wrote about cock and said this
Charles Dickens wrote about Christmas and said this

They all said this -

Ahrrrrrrr!
(to be shouted really fucking loud).

Why The Privileged Need To Read Literature
By Camillus John

The privileged piss on the homeless on Henry Street.
The privileged punch drunks and junkies
out of their way leaving shops.
The privileged can't understand why anyone
would have to sign on the dole.
The privileged can't abide to live
within one hundred miles of any travellers.
The privileged judge people
from certain areas
with racist stereotypes.

Which is why the privileged need to
read literature more than the poor,
to ameliorate the lack of empathy
for other people
they splash preciously about within
on a day to day basis.
Books, books and even more books.
Get it into them.
And into them.
And into them.

The not-so-privileged look at
all the people of the above,
with some sort of understanding,
which is why their need
for as much literature
as the privileged
is not so pressing,
yet lots of them
read but

not enough write.
Books, books and even more books.
Get it into them.
And into them.
And into them.

The Two Spongers
By Ciara MacDermott

I should have lied. The LOTTO ticket was gripped by my mean fisticuffed hands. A prom queen I may have been 40 years ago, but what a haggard old cow I was now. My husband Joe left our Sacramento 3 bedded semi-detached home 14 months ago but I still missed the cheating swine.

The phone call I made to him 45 minutes ago maybe done the trick to reel him back into my deceitful web of lies. Maybe I should have lied and told him that I didn't play my regular 7 numbers in the state lottery. Like every other week, except for Sunday. But as soon as I got a missed call from him, I knew the slimy little rat wanted to know if I had played my usual numbers. He had seen them on his flat screen LCD tv that Miranda had bought him. That wretched little bitch! Wait till I get my hands on her!!!

So like the fool I had always been I phoned Joe back and told him I had played my usual numbers. Then explaining to him that I'd won the whole 68 million dollars in the lottery. That would set him straight. Or would it?

His red Lamborghini beeped with prestigious timing outside my white picket fences at my garden gates. That shallow little whore plopped her curvy Latino behind out of the leather interior of the car like the Imperial Empress of Japan. Plopping along on the pavement with her Jimmy Choo stiletto heels like a duck to water, she waddled up to my front door with Joe. The audacity of that uncultured little cow, but I'd make her feel my wrath soon enough.

As the two spongers sat on my cream leather mahogany edged couches, sipping on the wine I gave them with crackers and cheese I busied myself in the kitchen, presumably to make them dinner, or so they thought!

My leather strapped belt was on my lap as I sat on my green cushioned stool in my kitchen. The Martha Stewart cookware set was my best bet for my mission ahead. With eager venom I sharpened my four best sharp-edged carving knives just in case.

You never knew with Joe and his plump tummy and ass cheeks. He could be mighty hard to carve through. As the two unbeknown idiots squealed and giggled amongst one another about the tv program on tv. I made my best effort to get the job done. Measuring my lino clear plastic bags ready for carving the little squirmy fuckers up.
Joe's $3000 dollar Armani suit was gonna be brown bread or more like tomato sauce. Bringing in the carved duck with apple sauce, roast potatoes and broccoli and carrots. They both tucked into their dinner.
Then from behind I slit their two throats. Marta's best carving knives engulfed in my beautifully manicured hands. The squirmy noises that came from their mouths nearly knocked me off track. But I had to get the job done.
Quickly placing the clear plastic lino bags on the floor all around the sofa they sat on. Their bodies trembled with the terror and shock that left their bodies eventually. Job well done Sharon. Beautifully well done honey!

Reclaiming My Power
By Ciara McDermott

You can't take my power away from me. You fucker! For as long as I live, I will still flock my sheep upon these moors for as long as I can breathe. Saffron Cagney was my married name, but since my divorce I've reclaimed my Ms O'Keefe. Those beguiling eyes of Tom Cagney which sparked both confusion and mischief within me 15 years ago are now gone.

Leaving the courthouse two weeks ago, I can still hear his screams. "You wretched woman Saffron Cagney. I'll be coming for you." But standing in my green trench coat soaked to the skin and tartan red checked trousers. My thoughts are how I am going to get the little swine into my sweaty palms.

I called a truce over the phone earlier that morning. He's to be arriving at 8pm sharp. So, I take my overalls, trench coat and sweaty wet clothes off. The pot of coddle in the kitchen is brewing. After my shower and washing the grime off me, I brush my cotton soft blonde hair.

The twine at the main door, I flick with my long manicured pink nails. "Wait till you see this, babycakes, I've got some goodies for you!" Chopping the sausage for the coddle and popping it into the pot. My mind gets thinking "What am I gonna do with his sausage?"

The doorbell rings and Pocahontas, my shiatzu, keeps barking after doing a wee and a nice fresh shit on the floor!!

Then the swine Tom walks in, as smirky as ever. "Hi sweetheart, how are you?" I grimace towards him. Before he can answer he falls on his snot right on top of the gooey fresh shit that Pocahontas just plonked out.

"What a great start!" I shout out loud. The twine works then the bonus gooey shit right in his face. He's out cold for five minutes.

This gives me time to wrap Tom up in my mothers old sailors ropes from the cupboard. Then as he's conked out, I get the urge to have a poop. Then returning to the crime scene afterwards, Tom's beginning to wake up. He finally wakes up and I start to feed him the lactose tablets to release the shit from his bowels and anus.

Then slowly I begin to chop up his underarms and the full length of his forearms and then his legs and ankles. Screaming at the top of his lungs, I gag him up. My plastic white overalls are really standing the test of time.

Finally after chopping up Toms ribcage, his ass-cheeks and golly-wog bits! I wipe my brow and have a fresh cup of Barrys' tea. He's not getting any of this land off me now. Then the meat mincing machine is going full hog. I fill the grimy fuckers bodymeat and fat into the meat mincing machine. The next morning his mam, Jemima comes for breakfast. "A full Irish breakfast! Oh Saffron, this breakfast is amazing! The black pudding is to die for!!!" "Oh thanks Jemima, it's from a local producer I recently sourced. Yummy yummy in my tummy" I reply. "Hahaha! Hahaha!"

With love and kisses, Saffron.

 ♥ X ♥ X

The Derelict House
By Ciara McDermott

I ran for a mile until I saw the brown derelict house. The deer were outside, rummaging through the grass devouring the fruit of their labours. As the sun glinted through the blades of grass, the cockerel in the field beside the derelict house was crowing to his heart's content. The smell of tobacco lingered in the air as if smoking from the chimney of a pipe. Next the chuckling of a man's voice caught my attention and froze me in my tracks.

As the hair on the back of my neck rose, so did the level of my attention. In his Welsh accent, he asked me what I was doing on his land. I told him that I was camping out for the night, and I got startled by a stranger lurking in the woods near my campsite.

He told me not to be so silly and that things like that didn't happen out in this neck of the woods.

Then my mind raced back to that awful event – being trapped in the lair of a strange stalker. It was like he was stalking the woods, waiting for his next prey to arrive. Thinking to myself, I thought "I'm not going to be your next meal, shithead, I'm outta here" And as quick as I could shake a lambs tail, I darted out of this strangers visual range as fast as I could.

To my amazement he didn't pant as he ran after me, for what felt like an eternity but was about twenty minutes.

The old man smoking his tobacco pipe knocked me out of my reverie and fantasy, asking me if I had lost my marbles. He was wondering why I hadn't spoken for the last few minutes.

I apologised, like a well brought up Irish girl telling the old man that I was reminiscing about what had happened to me, that had brought me to this point.

"I'm Jessica Ellis," I said, telling the old man in my sweet Galway accent; holding out my hand for him to grasp. He held my hand with the firmest grip I'd felt for a long time, especially for a man who looked like he was in his mid-seventies.

"My name is Tom Delaney" he said. "My father was Irish, my ma from the Welsh valleys, that's where the name comes in." "Oh I see," I said, trying not to look too nosy even though I was brimming with curiosity about this man.

He brought me into his derelict house which was surprisingly warm and cosy with logs burning on the fire. My mind lost again with the flickering of the fire, I returned back to that fateful event from only forty minutes ago. But yet it felt like a lifetime ago.

As I was running from this lunatic, I could smell the embers from the fire, raising up into the night sky. The clamping of the buckles on his boots, whacking against the rocky and muddy terrain. "Now what have we here?" was all I could hear, as a hand grabbed my shoulder with the fiercest grip. "You're a pretty little thing, aren't you?" he said as he forced his bodyweight on top of my full torso. I could feel the linen of my shirt deepen into the muddy ground.

I kicked him in the rocks as I pulled with all my might to come to my feet, running as fast as my breath could take me.

Until I finally saw the derelict house in the distance. A knock on the door of the house took me out of my reverie as a familiar voice asked "Where's the girl, Da?" To my startled surprise I turned around and the scruffy mongrel was there, dripping wet from the mud.

The Three Vixens
By Ciara McDermott

The fingertips of that slimy bastard were cropping up from beneath the moist, crumbly, clammy, sweaty soil. Taking my shovel I whacked the fecker's purple crusted hands back down beneath the soil. His fingertips were nice and crispy waiting to be munched upon, but I had no time for that tonight. There were a houseful of guests, 8 to be exact, on their way to dinner.

"Back to you later, Jeremy, you crummy ol' corpse of a man" I popped myself like the Easter bunny up the stairs to the bathroom, tearing my clothes off. Then stepping into the steamy, moist, running waterfall of water the scummy, grimy, stench of Jeremy's decaying, rotting, skeletal remains washing off my skin. Popping on the music on my stereo in my bedroom, I took out my red satin dress with black cape readying myself for the upcoming storm of anxious guests. Then slipping on my silky dernier and tights, g-strings sculpted my voluptuous cheeks, brassiere comatosing my wobbly knockers. Those guests were paying top dollar for this experience so might as well make the most of it.

After a cuppa cha, Deirdre and Allison dropped into the house with their spare set of keys in hand. "Right love, we've got the poles ready for popping, where do you want us love?"

"Eh how about over there beside the fireplace, me knockers are getting frosty" Twenty minutes later the three poles were set up for the three vixens in waiting. Waiting for their voluptuous cheeks to wobble like dynamite off the cold metal steel bars.

"Ding dong" the doorbell rang and the punters were unfolding upon the space in the main lounge area. Disco balls, music, red and white candles lit, the velvet couches with gold brass buttons embellished upon them, glinted against the red hot fire.

As the drinks were flowing from glass to mouths between these eight burly brazing working class men, so did the merriness.

The three vixens wobbled their chubby cheeks against the steel metal poles.

Winter
By Ciara McDermott

The speckles of snow glimmered through the windows as frost of the sky frosted the window pane.

The sun crackled through the clouded morning as if hoping and willing for a new day to begin.

The robin perched his twinkly toes on the outer edge of the window pane.

The tractors were revving up their engines readying themselves for the mornings feed for the hungry frost-bitten cows laying in the sheds.

The ferns edges shook off the specks and granules of snow as the robin jumped off his invisible trampoline and onto the fern's edge.

The foxes were burrowing in packs of two at a time sneakily hiding the treasures of gold, for after the melting of the winter's snow.

The hooves of the horse's shoes could be heard clinking along the tarmacadam as the ridges pressed the inner thighs onto the outer and under stomach of the horse's torso.

The red berries glistened in the background along the edge of the road hitting the riders flat on the head as they went on their merry way.

The carol singers kept singing to their hearts content even to the dismay of the unwavering audience. The fluffy top bonnets bouncing on their heads as they enthusiastically sang like a cherry bird waiting for its reward.

With due course they got their hot cross buns steaming with melted butter and a hot cup of tea. The audience wilfully gave them their prize to quickly push them along their way.

The sheep ruffled their fluffy, curly coats, to release them of the snowy clumps of restraint. The young ewes were baaaahing for their mothers' warm milk and cosy cuddles of warmth. Clamouring past one another for their mother's attention.

Finally subdued from their warm feeds and cosy cuddles

The baby ewes floated into a deep sleep and off to sleepy, dreamy winterland.

The cocks were crowing with their shiny glossy coats, sparkling with autumny wintery dew.
Their long-manicured toenails clicked and scraped the soil as they rummaged for the winters feed.

Freedom
By David Moroney

Greater than the angels,
Masters of the earth,
What a holy privilege
Bestowed upon the earth
Made in the likeness, of the holy one above,
Sharing in his glory,
The future is pure love.

My Friend John
By David Moroney

I saw him first in the park. He surely was a real bright spark. So cool and calm but sharp and brisk. Good looking too, quick with his fists.

New to the gang, but not afraid. It wasn't long before he got laid.

The years went by.

You foolish boy, out of the way, you're only a toy. His mouth was big, his words were fast, he thought he came out of a special caste. Now drugs came on the scene you know. And it became all go.

Years went by.

Highs and Lows, the subtle evil struck its blows. The coolest kids on the block became addicted to more than just pot. Now when is it going to end? Not soon to my dear friends. Now of course there were the ones who saw it coming and soon they all started running. Cool John and I were left behind. He became my friend, don't you mind.

Well really who would have us? A pair of beasts in a rut. High and low to the bitter end, time to part from my dear friend.

Years went by.

I found my way but my old friend continued to sway. But then the day came anew, my old friend came through. First on the street in a brief encounter, after then in a hostel where he worked as a bouncer. I spoke a little to my old friend. He hadn't changed, he didn't mend. The years had passed but not for John. He never grew beyond the harm.

So our encounters kept up but sadly I saw he was messed up. The pain, the hurt, the damage was done. Nervous breakdowns made him numb. Medication to ease the pain, reality beyond his gain.

We met quite often, I made a point, the friendship was different, not about a joint. His pride was hurt beyond the pain, no one to talk to, no one to explain.

The years passed by. I kept in touch. We hadn't much to say. Silence was enough. I called him this day. "I'll pick you up" When I saw him coming, I was struck. John, you don't look well. You got so thin."My head is wrecked" replied from within.

He moved from a hostel to his own private flat. A high ideal, but a lonely trap. We met once or twice, shortly after that. Not much better was my friend with the hat.

He spoke once or twice, rare enough for John, and was even honest, it was like a bomb. My mother said 'You should see a Doctor, you don't look well', he nodded like an actor.

The weeks passed by. I returned home one day. Two women in the kitchen, who are they? Hello. I'm Johns sister. Found dead in his flat. It fitted the picture. What happened I asked. We don't really know. The police said 'A mystery' but I don't think so.

John'd had enough. Life took its toll. The mental anguish no more could he hold. Oh God when I look back with guilt and shame, no use in dwelling on that fruitless pain. Much is given, much you expect, but for one who got little, surely mercy respects.

Padre Pio
By David Moroney

Man of God 'a big following' man of God. What have you got that others don't 'chosen one' man of God. They flocked to you to hear their woes; you kept them all on their toes. Not all was softness and shallow love, a firm word from above. Confession box day and night to bring some peace to their strife. Little sleep, little rice, man of prayer paid the price. So much was done for me you said, from the man on the cross who is the head. In heaven now you suffered long but now you sing the heavenly song. Not forgotten, never rest help us Pio be our best.

The pope has come
By David Moroney

The pope has come; it will be fun, who is this man from the Roman sun. I give you keys, thy will be done, friend or foe, let it go. What gain'th on earth will be in heaven, what lose'th on earth you lose in heaven, oh my God a frightening thought to lose salvation, Jesus bought.

Now now not so rash a simply yes for dog and cat, but not for humans who like the cash. The pope has come so let's get ready, he drives in a Skoda and likes spaghetti. This man of God, what will he say? your all in trouble change your way. What happened to all the saints and scholars? They travelled the world but not for dollars.

Ok, ok we messed up too, says he to us, yes it's true. I'm a man, just like you, I .get it wrong, what will I do. The scandals within the church of Christ, a wound a sore a mighty blight. What went wrong, what did we do in the name of the Lord, how could this be true?

Power corrupts, more power too, such respectable forms, so subtle too, a hand shake here, a smile there, a nod and a wink without moving a chair. What more can I say, that hasn't been said, except turn to God who is the head, the mighty one, who sees all, loving and forgiving for all who call.

Remember that day, Lord; in the sand, the woman to be stoned by the righteous man, trembling and dread, ready to die, this woman you know called out her last cry. Now here there, before you go, the man without sin, make the first throw. Where are they gone? Not one left, just you and me adulteress; you are free to go, you are forgiven, no more stray to the sin that's forbidden.

Weary
By David Moroney

Weary so weary hungry and all, what's it all about this life of call.
The opportunities given, the blind lead the blind in a constant rhythm.
More and more let's explore; this bottomless pit of empty chore,
seek it here, seek it there, worldly charms that have no core.
Never ending ceaseless search, for what can't satisfy the human thirst.
I want it now, I want it now what others have, I want that cow.
Jealous, envy the root of all, cause of many to fall.
The battle is on, who'll win the race, don't even try without some faith.
It's up to me, it's up to you, sought and find, what is true.

Declan Geraghty was born and raised in Dublin. He's an actor, short story writer and novelist. He studied theatre under director Caroline McSweeney where he played the title role in the Patrick Marber play Howard Katz. Declan has also written and acted in a devised work of Pirandello's Six Characters Searching for an Author in the Crypt theatre.

He also wrote and performed his own monologues in the Designyard for renowned performance artist Oscar McLennon. Other works included parts in Tosca in the Gaiety theatre directed by Dietmar Pfegerl. He's completed various short films in Ireland and Spain and worked with Paula Vallepuga and the Desvaraciones theatre group in Madrid.

Declan is a fluent Spanish speaker and lived in Madrid for over ten years where he taught English. His first published short story, Seagulls, was included in the 2017 short stories collection Dublin in the Coming Times.

He was part of the InkSplinters anthology of 2018, and his most recent work was a Collection of short stories and poems alongside broadcaster Joe Duffy, singer songwriter Declan O'Rourke and novelist Neville Thompson. Which was entitled the Flying Superhero Clothes Horse.
He is one of two founding members of the Ballyfermot writers' group alongside Camillus John.

At the moment he is working on a collection of his own short stories and a novel and hopes to publish them in the near future. He currently resides in Clondalkin and has a chip on his shoulder that gets bigger by the hour.

Alcoholic
By Declan Geraghty

Alcohol sprinkles
Alcohol days
Alcohol everything
Alcohol to get through the day
Alcohol the coping mechanism
Alcohol the sea
Alcohol the sun
Alcohol the cure
Alcohol the hangover
Alcohol here
Alcohol there
Alcohol everywhere
Alcohol dates
Alcohol sex
Alcohol dreams
Alcohol DTs
Alcohol break
Alcohol rehabilitation
Alcohol liver
Alcohol death
Alcohol kids
Alcohol now
Alcohol broke up my family
Alcohol socially
Alcohol all day
Alcohol religion
Alcohol excuses
Alcohol arguments
Alcohol fights

Augusta 2. 71
By Declan Geraghty

He came to Augusta 2. 71.
The Jewish man from the past.
The Jewish man from the future
The adverts flickered and the Flymys flew overhead with obsessed and awestruck eyes. The crowds gathered from everywhere. As minutes passed there was no traffic, just a mass standstill.

For an Arabic man. An Arabic man with a handsome face.
An Arabic man with unkempt hair and unshaven.
An Arabic man talking about equality.
An Arabic man talking about sharing all that we have and giving to each other.
And they roared.

And the Police couldn't help but roar with them. And the stock market started to collapse. Cries could be heard. As the people realised what was happening in the system of el Capitalismo as it used to be known.

And they cried. They cried at there stupidity. And the pope came to Augusta 2. 71 and he looked onto Jesus and said.
"This is not a man. This is the son of god.
More powerful than the stars and all the angels."

_____

_____

_____

_____

Then   there   was   silence

_____

_____

And the people cried, they cried, then screamed in ecstasy

there would be

a   new   beginning _____ A   beginning   without
mortgages and putting people on the edge of poverty. A beginning free
of a rat race to consume and reflect vanity with currency.

And Jesus smiled and was never seen again

The new way was to live and have all necessary work done through
cooperation and communication,but most of all through understanding
and compassion.

And with a sprinkling of love for one another.
Augusta 2. 71 was never the same again

And they were happy

And it was good.

Black Rain
By Declan Geraghty

Rain
Black rain
The type that destroys your clothes and dirties the cars
The type that makes you ill
The black rain of Dublin
It makes Dublin even dirtier than ever
Dirty Dublin swimming in the black rain
The black rain falls on Violeta's head as she holds my hand
The rain is not black when it touches her
And even in the Dublin black rain she is happy and playing
Mischievous in the damp
A moving rainbow in the cascade of dull
I heard a guy hung himself in Neilstown this morning
He was just eighteen
The black rain can push people over the edge sometimes
It's a Dublin thing the Black rain

Dedicated to Mark O'Kelly
Rest in peace

Knowing Paula
By Declan Geraghty

Paula why didn't I know you when I was twenty?

Why couldn't I have bumped into you somehow?

We met each other at the most difficult time in our lives

like a metaphorical drug to soothe the pain of living.

You are a beautiful woman inside and out

A poem can't do you Justice

Your green eyes give me hope but they also make me feel vulnerable

Stay with me a little longer Paula.

Dedicated to Paula McLoughlin

Open the box
By Declan Geraghty

Open the box with the key

Pull back the lid then smell inside the box

Almost tasting its moisture and fragrance

Take it in as much as you can until your senses are not enticed any more

Put it down, gently, lovingly then close the lid

Turn the key and lock it.

Come back to the box another day

And open and smell it in a different way.

Scum
By Declan Geraghty

Garda O'Sheas Friday night blowjob at the canal wasn't as pleasing as usual. A new brazzer was on tonight. Sinead was her name. Fucking junkie he thought. He made his way up to Blakey in Ringsend. He had money to collect off that scrawny little drug dealing cunt. If he wanted to keep his patch he'd have to cough up like the horrible skinny little bastard he was. He walked up Pearse street then up past Shelbourne park, it was a lovely summers evening. Not even the need for a cardigan, sure ye could be in Spain it's that nice thought O'Shea.

He collected his money off that little prick Blakey. He looked more strung out than usual but fuck him we all had overheads, there was no sense being a cunt about it. O'Shea decided to fuck off for a quick pint in the Yacht. The clientele wasn't up to his standard thought the old guard. Fucking scumbags all these Dubs. He sipped his pint and reminisced about the kingdom. The rolling green hills of Kerry. Ahhhh paradise. Ah great memories all the same he sighed, not like this shithole.

Ringsend! Dublin's sewer, the electricity plant plus the waste incinerator. Not to mention the shit treating plant which treated over one million peoples shit before pumping it out into Dublin Bay where come summertime the dirty cunts would be swimming in it. Wankers!

O'Shea felt his prostate tinkle and quickly rushed to the jacks. He went into a cubicle as he was always a little bit shy about pissing in the shanks alongside other men. As he began to piddle, he realised that with his ever-increasing beer belly he couldn't see his penis anymore. Years of greed and overeating he pondered. The old country mentality of it's ok to be a fat cunt. Sure ya need a bit of weight on ye boyo. His old man said to him in his head.

At least he wasn't an anorexic like that dying looking cunt Blakey. Sure, ya need a bit of meat on your bones Lad! His mother's high-pitched screech repeated to his inner chi. He ordered another pint of Guinness and began reminiscing again, this time about his old flame Sandy. She was a recurring tale, especially for the boys down in the station. Ohh I tell ye lads O'Shea would always recall. She'd legs like a fooking west Cork heifer and by Jaysus a fooking set a tits to go with them.

As he looked into the distance at nothing in particular, he caught a glimpse of a scowling Blakey in the bar mirror in front of him. He then saw two huge flashes of light. He heard screaming and could only see the ceiling. He knew he was dying. That fucking sneaky cunt Blakey he tried to mutter.

THEN DARKNESS

COMPLETE SILENCE

What felt like an eternity. He eventually opened his eyes. There was an awful smell. He realised he was in a pigsty. He couldn't talk only squeal. He squealed for hours and hours with all the other little piglets until it was nighttime and all the other animals went to sleep, but the farmer didn't hear him. He eventually drifted off to sleep on the tit of a huge sow. Ah well! Fuck it! at least I'm back down the country he thought.

The Wave
By Declan Geraghty

Give me a bit of that wave
It washes over me like cool Spanish air in a July heatwave
Give me a bit of that look you give when your thinking
You think things the boys in the council estates might never comprehend
Give me a bit of that conversation
When I go home and think in depth of what you meant when you said this or that
Show me how to do those decisions
Responsible and thoughtful ones, ones that always went over my head
Learn us some of that grammar
That grammar I never got a hold of
Let's see a bit of that style you have
A style that comes natural to you
A style that can't be bought
A style that can't be found with a credit card and a gay best friend
A style I feel intimidated by and disconnected from
Give us a bit of the sound of your accent
It soothes my nerves
My Dublin nerves
Always fidgeting
Getting the eye from this cunt or that
Will you give me a bit of your passion
I don't see it in you enough
Only when you're angry
Gimme a bit of you
Just be you
I like you a lot
I don't want anything
Well maybe just to sit back in my own personal admiration of you
That's about it really

No double barrelled answers
Nor profound rebuttals
No swapping innuendos
Just a yes or a no
Or an I'm happy, I'm sad kind of acknowledgement
Can I see you for you someday?

Welcome to the game
By Declan Geraghty

What I write is not for your eyes.
It was never intended for you, yet here you are reading it.
Here you are eating it up,
Drinking it.
Were you meant to read it?
Was it destiny that you read it or did you do it on purpose?
Is it just the drugs talking?
Is it the drugs thinking?
Maybe it just happened accidentally that your reading this.
You kind of just, came across it.
You came across it and took it in.
You came across it and took it in for some reason unbeknown to you.
And as your walking down the street now.
This shit is suddenly in your mind now.
Then you ask yourself why do writers write?
You keep walking then you forget about it.
Then a few weeks later you think about what I wrote.
And it's somehow still in your head.
Then you add it all up.
Now you kind of know why.
I think you always knew.
Didn't you?

The Eight Sisters
By Diarmuid Fitzgerald

(after Trish Nugent)

Eight shot glasses are placed in a row for eight sisters.
I fill the middle six half way up with vodka, pure and unmixed.
The last two glasses at either end I fill right to the top.
Five of my sisters come to collect their glasses.
We clink them and drink to our health
and renew out silent vows — to love, fight, gossip, and support.
The shots are downed.
The last two glasses are left until the end.
We pass them around and drink in memory of Joan and Annette.
A five minute cry is allowed and we let the salty water come then go.

Prayer
By Diarmuid Fitzgerald

God's grandeur in
a steeple appearing over a hill
a rose hip bud in this early spring
a sudden opening in the hedgerow
a breeze blowing dust from the path
a click clack sound of walking poles
a sun-wheel coming through the clouds
a green field that seems to go on and on
a leaf from an olive tree brushing the wind
a sharp turn in the path as it zig-zags down a slope

A Sort of Song
By Diarmuid Fitzgerald

What can I say but say the same thing
everyone else has said?
The swan and swallow sing of the dying day.
Leaves drop and wither, the river slurps on.
The sun goes down as nature shrugs.
I come home to a room where
I do not hear my family far, far from
this new land of neon, rush and crowds.
Staying at home all day is very fine
but it will not serve me any good
nor bring a crowd of friends near.
Maybe I can say something in my own way
but if so who will notice my song?

Faltering into Sound
By Diarmuid Fitzgerald

The hanger half moves on the pole
casting a rainbow light around the room.
I plough through the early poems
of faltering grace of a poet

now worthy of great praise.
In hopeful comparison
I try to find my rung
on a ladder of failures and compromises.

In that turning delicacy, I wonder
if I can do more than skim a stone of words
across the surface,
that when I call the language comes.

Like the deep muffle of my breath,
a hemmed skirt ruffling down the stairs,
a drunken man reaching for light.
The slack curtains shielding the night's freeze.

Outside the hanger tilts again in the breeze.
I push my hand against a wall
of straining silence
to make an indentation of sound.

Benedición
By Diarmuid Fitzgerald

May the clouds come between you and the sun.
May the path stay dry and solid.
May the walk spare you blisters.
May the bag on your back be easy to carry.
May the shops open on time.
May the wine and beer be reasonable.
May the locals stay friendly.
May the showers in the Albergues work.
May the snorers find another room.
May the rains come during the night.

Meeting Luis
By Diarmuid Fitzgerald

It was his photo that attracted me. His online profile said he was honest, liked a laugh and wanted to meet someone sincere. I got in touch by email and then we swapped numbers. We texted back and forth and then I asked him to meet up. Luis agreed and I let him decide on the location. He gave me a sense that he was a man who knew his own tastes. I imagined him picking a place where the food would be gorgeous and the location beautiful.

We arranged to meet in a café near St. James's Hospital. I was not familiar with that area. It was awkward for me to get to. I worked on the other side of the city. Luis said it was a great café. In fact, it was a very ordinary place with Formica tabletops, Lino floor, and cheap leather chairs.

Luis looked exactly like his photo: black hair, tanned skin, thick eyebrows, and a slender face.

'Good to meet you?' I said.
'The same here.'

I immediately liked the way he slurred his s's in his soft Spanish voice.

'How was your day?' Luis asked.
'Fine. Busy.'

I didn't want to talk about work or the dramas there.

'What do you do?' Luis asked.
'I work in an office.'

I felt my heart sink and hoped Luis would not ask any follow-up questions about work. It was then I noticed that Luis was dressed rather shabbily. His coat was a little dirty and his shoes were well worn. I hoped he wasn't poor.

Luis chatted animatedly with the waitress in Spanish. She noticed me and smiled and turned back. Luis's hands were moving about in the air as were the waitresses. They kissed each other on the cheeks. I felt a rush of jealousy come over me. Maybe it was pettiness on my part. After all the continental types are super intimate with each other. A kiss on the cheek is just a hello in their language. Soon the waitress moved off and served some other customers.

'What would you like?' Luis asked.

I was delighted that Luis was offering to pay. Maybe he wasn't that poor after all.

'A latte please,' I responded.
'Lattes are bad for the waist. Too many calories.'
'An Americano then.'
'Much better choice.'

I was a little annoyed by Luis for giving me this advice. However, he was good looking so maybe he did have a point. Looking down, I saw that my belly came over my belt. He was of slim build so I should follow his advice.

The waitress took our order. Soon I heard the banging of pots and the hiss of steam. Luis had his phone out and he was flicking through it. This went on for some time. I was getting restless now. It was quite rude that Luis was on his phone. I was even thinking of getting up and walking when he put his phone away.

'I'm very sorry to have done that. You see my mum in Spain is having an operation today and my sister is posting updates.'
'I am sorry to hear that she is ill.'
'She had problems with her gallbladder over the years. I told her to go to the doctors about it but she kept putting it off. Eventually, she did and she got sent to the hospital. The operation is happening today. I'm nervous.'
'I bet you are.'
'How's your own family?' Luis asked.
'Fine, as far as I can tell.'

A guilty feeling came over me. It was a long time since I even asked my siblings or my parents about their health. These days I don't talk to them that much.

'So what do you do for a living?' I asked to move the conversation on.
'I'm a student. I'm over here for a year on an Erasmus program.'
'Do you like it?'
'The weather is often cold. So much rain and so little sun.'

Luis said the 'so's' with a pained expression.

'At least it's hot in Spain,' I said.
'We get really nice weather. Just enough sun to keep it really hot.'

Our coffees arrived and the waitress beamed a big smile at Luis. He said something to her in Spanish. She smiled even more. They chatted a little bit in more animated tones. I was really annoyed now. Finally, she went away. We sipped our coffees. I was thinking about moving the conversation onto holidays when Luis broke the silence.

'Your face is beautiful when it's not cross.'

I was dumbstruck. Anger came over me.

'That was not a nice thing to say.'
'Sorry if I hurt you. I was hoping you would smile more.'
'I smile when I am happy,' I said.

Luis was making things worse. He had transgressed a line and insulted my appearance. He must apologise for this.

'You could say sorry for making such a comment.'
'I did say sorry. I didn't mean to be rude.'

There was a long pause in our conversation.

'So,' Luis said in a tone that was an octave higher, 'what exactly do you do in work?'
'It's an office job. Lots of typing and emailing.'
'A nice job?'
'Not really. It's just work.'

More silence. I finished my coffee and wondered if I should order more. The last thing I needed was to bring the waitress back with her flirty smiles. Luis was only about half way through his espresso. He must be a slow drinker. That's probably a good thing. Someone told me that everyone eats and drinks too fast nowadays.

'Nice day outside,' I said to break the silence.
'It's not too bad.'
'What do you do outside of studying?'
'I enjoy the city and its people. The people here are very friendly, just like Spain.'
'Dublin people can be quite rude.'
'Sure like anywhere but overall Dublin people are genuine and helpful.'
'Dublin is not a nice city.'
'Really,' Luis nearly shouted out, 'I love it here. It's great.'
'The city is filthy. So much begging goes on.'

'There is a lot of begging here. But it's still great. The music here is fantastic.'

I don't know much about the music scene here as I don't go out that much. Luis was really nice I decided. I wondered did Luis have his own room? I had to ask him in an indirect way. If I was too direct then I might scare him off.

'So do you live with others or on your own?'
'I share an apartment with three others near here. It's very small.'
'At least you have your own room.'
'Actually, I share it with Fabio.'
'Oh with another guy!'
'There is nothing going on between me and Fabio. It's just that rent is so expensive here in Dublin. The only way I can afford to rent a place is by sharing my room.'
'I've never shared a room. Even when I was a child I had my own room.'
'Lucky for you!'
'Do you mind sharing a room?'
'It's OK. I'm used to it I guess. It's a learning.'

I was puzzled by his expression. Maybe Luis's grasp of English was not that great.

'What do you mean by, "It's a learning"?'
'I mean it's like a life lesson.'
'Oh, I see.'

Luis was about two-thirds through his coffee. Was he slow with his food? I would find it unbearable to be with someone who was slow about everything they did. A fast pace is my preference. The waitress came back all smiles. Maybe she had unbuttoned another button in her blouse. I could see the tops of her breasts through the open V. As she leaned over to clear away my cup I caught Luis gazing down the V. Luis chatted away with her again. Perhaps he was arranging a date with her? I folded my arms and could feel my brow tense. This brings up my wrinkles and I do not like that at all.

'Have you been on other dates?' I asked suddenly.
'Yes, quite a few with guys and with girls.' Luis added with a cool tone.
'Both men and women,' I shouted out.
'Yes, both. I'm bisexual.'
'You're one of those!'

Luis slammed down his coffee cup and looked at me with a hard face.

'I think that was a bit rude, don't you think?'
'Rude. I'm shocked that's all. You don't look bisexual.'

Luis let out a whistle and put his hands on his head.

'I can't believe I am hearing this. I get so much judgment.'
'Sorry if I hurt you in any way.'
'Ok, Ok.'

Total silence. Luis being a bisexual is a problem for me. It means he would be looking over his shoulder at every man or woman around.

'As an act of apology I'll pay for the coffee,' I offered.
'There's no need. You said sorry and I accept it. I need to go to the bathroom.'

Luis got up quickly. It felt that he was trying to get away. I'll have to mind my tongue in the future. After a while, Luis came out of the toilet and went up to the cash register. I made my way up and motioned to the waitress that I wanted to pay.

'Are you paying together?' she inquired.
'Separate.' Luis said.

I took that as a sign that Luis was not interested in me anymore. I paid after him. We both headed to the door and stepped outside. Luis turned around and smiled at me.

'It was nice to meet you, Derek. I hope you have a great week.'
'Yes, it was nice to meet you too Luis. It would be nice to catch up again?'

Luis just smiled. We shook hands. I found the tightness of his grip reassuring. Maybe he didn't hate me after all. Hopefully, all would be forgiven. Luis turned sharply and walked away with his footsteps stepping over the coloured litter as he went.

Normal
By Dylan Henvey

The fence has rust, the line has rotten,
Still storm clouds come close,
To scatter the sands and scourge the coast.
The inlet howls, must all innocence fall fowl?
Who heard the whispers of those afraid to speak?
Who silenced the ones who never could?
Beauty is only skin deep
Well then skin me alive!
Where has vanity left to hide?
Sanity, cannot be recognised in a house of madness
Unbalanced
Unrestrained
Unhinged, and tinged with sadness.

The alliteration of the obliteration of love
By Dylan Henvey

A love forged from benevolent plans, pathetically pitters in the palm of
your hand
Banish bitter bow
Anxious arrow break
Blossom from the loss, found beyond the quake
Sallow scented sands
Reeling scorched earth
Gleaming gloom, terrified tides, gleaming gloom gone berserk.
Wild warriors wither
The menacing meek masquerade
Thumping hearts harrow heroes, a ragged renaissance reigns.
It took so long; it took so long, to find a pedestal worthy of putting you
on
It took so long; it took so long, to find a pedestal worthy of putting you
on

Hencho
By Dylan Henvey

Hencho, in his hearts rush was a rogue, palpitation personified; his burly body bulged through his tight Imitation Italian suits. Thick powerful hands protruded from his sleeves, always wanting, always waiting for some barbarous act, or brutal deed. He had a distinct high pitch Irish brogue, especially when riled. Most of the time, his voice was as effeminate as I have ever heard from any man, almost sweet. However, it gave a grave eerie aura in its deliverance, for it could never fully vail the violent torrent surging beneath the surface. Hencho was heinous and abhorrent, yet honoured and adored in equal measure. The Libertine of the liberties, Hencho loved women and women loved Hencho. As charming and as seductive and as deathly as a cigarette. Hencho oozed class when the world was watching. A smokescreen, Old school, a smile could stick as long as was needed, a gentleman in his own mind. I hated him! Yet never forgot that First and foremost, he was as formidable and as ferocious as any man in the city.

He Looked Different Somehow
By Dylan Henvey

He looked different somehow, bigger than I had imagined, maybe because my mother hung from his neck like a scarf. She showered him kisses as if each one would turn back the hands of the clock a tock at a time. My sister ran and jumped into his arms, he squeezed her so tight I was sure she'd scream, but she didn't, instead she held him even tighter. Me, well I just stood there and stared, I had always hoped this day would come, never believing it would and in disbelief it actually had. He was home, it was two weeks past my second Birthday when he left, now it was two months until my 7th, go and make me a cup of tea please love, oh how I've missed your tea, makes the best cup of tea in the world your ma

"Da, do you wanna see the new jig I learned in Irish Dancin?' my sister asked him excitedly

'Course I do honey, go get your shoes so I can have the full river dance experience'

'Ok Da' out she shot with a spark. Then he turned to me, I Stood still and silent, till this day my heart has never beaten so fast. He took off his Blue U.N. beret, placed it on my head with his left hand, then slapped it down as quick with his right 'well soldier I'm your father'

He shot up, straightened his back, saluted and roared PRESENT AND REPORTING FOR DUTY!!!

Nowhere fast
By Dylan Henvey

You get soaked to the bone at the bus stop, the bus finally comes, there's no seats, the bus breaks down, some scaldy balls starts shouting at the driver, some other scaldy balls starts shouting at him for shouting at the driver. Oddly enough it seems like I'm the only one not shouting. The word "poxy" is screeched back and forth in high pitched Dublin accents. The driver tries the engine for the dozenth time, 'cause god loves a trier. The driver is finally told to go back to his own country (which apparently is Pakistan but I think he's Spanish). Surly he doesn't intend for him to start this home coming journey immediately? Either way, we are going nowhere fast.

Comingstraightouttaballyer
By Dylan Henvey

The wealthy who keep horses are lauded, often offered great reverence, considered more cultured, deeper of character, perhaps holding an intuition, or at least a capability to understand, appreciate and love other creatures for their natural beauty at a level others fail to comprehend. (No, not bestiality.)

The poor who own horses are often sneered at, labelled knackers, pikeys, perhaps considered backward, uncultured . Incapable of caring for creatures that are not already dead southern fried and presented in a "bargain bucket". The fascination that has ignited such passion in men women and children for thousands of years to want to own, tame, love these creatures is sparked at the same basic level in all who it illuminates. Hands up! (that's a horsey joke) let's stop the discrimination against knackers with horses.

- If I get 10 likes I'll give one of the horses an apple. (It really needs the apple, it's been left out in the middle of a field in the rain and is extremely malnourished, not really being cared for correctly).

- if I get less than 7 I won't tell the young lads to stop when they jacket them down the path over broken glass.

- if I get less than 5 one of the horses will die. (Such is the power of face book likes.)

Erin Percival is a nine year old writer and violin player from lower Ballyfermot who sings and dances with C&S Variety Group in Cherry Orchard. She is also a cub scout and an excellent ping pong player, going by the name Professor Ping, but never ever, Pope Pong (that would be her uncle). This year she very much likes unicorns - and has got the handbag to prove it.

The Magic Tree 2 – The Pink Piano With Blue Stripes
By Erin Percival

Mia and I were in the woods. My Mum was getting us a surprise. We had to go out and play. To get out of her way. We went deep into the woods. Soon we realised we were lost. I forgot my phone so couldn't ring anyone for help. Mia said, "Wait, I have my phone with me." But when she checked her pocket it had disappeared. She said, "It must have fallen out along the way."

I tried to sort out a plan but was empty-minded and said, "Mia, have you any ideas yet?"

"Nope. Kate, I'm empty-headed too," said Mia.

We saw a woman walking through the woods towards us. We were petrified to ask her if she knew the way home because our mothers told us not to talk to strangers. We tried to hide but when the woman got closer it turned out she was actually my Mum - she was with our dog Pony! My Mum said, "Are you and Mia okay?' 'Yes, we are fine,' we said. But we were cold.

She took us back to the house for some hot chocolate. We warmed up. But then we remembered we'd forgotten to bring Pony with us. We rushed back to the woods but couldn't find poor old Pony anywhere. We rushed home and asked the magic tree, Frederick Hill, who lives in the park near our house. "Frederick, did you see our dog Pony anywhere?" The magic tree said, "Yes, I saw her with ten other dogs." He didn't know where though. "They were having a great time."

We went back in to the house and my Mum told us all about the surprise she had in store for us. It was a new house, a mansion. "And Kate, your friend Mia can sleep over tonight too!"
"Mum, when are we going to the new house? I can't wait."

"Tomorrow."

But then we got very sad because Pony was gone. Her food was uneaten in her silver bowl and her blanket was empty. That night Mia stayed in my house. While my Mum was sleeping, we sneaked downstairs at midnight and made slime to cheer ourselves up. At one o'clock we made Lost Dog posters for Pony to put up around the neighbourhood. Then we sneaked back up to bed.

We couldn't sleep. We were still worried about Pony. At 9.30 the next morning a knock came to the door. It was Pony! A miracle. Someone had found her and brought her home. We were delighted. She barked and told us all about the fun she had had with the other dogs in the woods. She was tired now and hungry. We got dressed and ate pancakes for breakfast to celebrate. Afterwards, we played with Pony for a while then my Mum came downstairs and took us to our new house. It was beautiful.

And can you believe it, there was another magic tree in our new back garden – she was our old magic tree's sister. She was our new magic tree. Her name was Melanie Hill. In the new house we had a new wardrobe, a new sofa, a new kitchen table, a new laptop, new beds and a new back garden - everything was new. My room was like a dream room. The house even had a separate room for Pony.

I went out to Melanie, the magic tree 2, in my new back garden to say hello and she gave me a book. It was like a dream book. It floated. Frederick Hill, the magic tree 1, and Melanie Hill, the magic tree 2, wrote it just for me and Mia using their branches for pencils.

As a result Mia and I stayed for four hours with Melanie. We played hide and seek. Even though Melanie couldn't move, she still found us.

Because she was magic. We also played Freeze-Tag and all sorts of different games.

Eventually, we had to go in and eat our dinners. Mia and I had skipped lunch as we were having so much fun. Before we left though, we asked Melanie if we could do it all over again tomorrow. She said, "Yep. Sure can."

The next morning I went downstairs and called for Mum. She wasn't anywhere to be seen. I knocked at Mia's house next door but nobody was there either. Melanie, the magic tree 2, was fast asleep in the back garden snoring. I didn't know what was happening.

Then suddenly my Mum was back.

I said, "Where have you been?"

My Mum said, "I got you a piano and it's coming tomorrow. It's pink with blue stripes." I was so happy. I said, "Wait. Why is there only a tomato for breakfast?"

"We've only got a tomato because Mia's Mum didn't do the shopping and took our food when I wasn't looking," said my Mum. Mia and her family now live next door to our new mansion.

"What are we meant to eat Ma? Hold on, I have a Wonka bar somewhere."

"No! You can't eat that for breakfast." said my Mum.

"Ok. Let's do the shopping," I said.
Finally food.

When we came back from the supermarket Melanie had two tickets for Ariana Grande waiting for me and Mia hanging from one of her branches. We were so excited.

Now we had to shop for clothes for the concert. We went to Pennys and got some really good stuff. I can't wait to wear them. When we got back to the house later, my new pink piano with blue stripes was floating in the living room. I was so excited. I sat down beside it in the air and played an Ariana Grande song.

Friendship
By Hazel Masterson

When you need me to be there for you, and don't understand that I can't, please don't give up on our friendship, I am not the person I used to be, in mind, body or soul. There is a reason for this, something that no one understands, I am doing my best day by day. Sometimes the real me is fighting to push through the never ending pain and exhaustion that is part of my daily life now. Some days are better than others. I embrace them with all my heart. On the bad days I feel my life is slipping away from me. I think about all the things I should and could be doing, example travelling, dancing, enjoying a night out with friends. Having to make excuses not to go out with you, because I cannot stay awake and the only way to stop the pain is to sleep! Our friendship is all that keeps me fighting each day, hoping someday I will be there for you again and enjoy all the fun times that we shared together. So please don't give up on our friendship. All I ask from you is patience, understanding and support with this invisible illness called -

That Summer In Dublin
By Hazel Masterson

Radio:
"The weatherman has just announced
Ireland is to have a heat wave,
a tropical heat wave, that could
possibly last four to six weeks."

Four Weeks Later

Jacinta:
Ah Jaysus Sharon, I never thought
dat I would be prayin fer rayin

Sharon:
I know Jacinta, sure it's only after costin'
me a fortune, between trips out on the
DART to the sea-side, ice cream, chips,
fizzy drinks, beach toys.

Sher it's alright for you, with no
bleedin' kids hanging outtya.

Try bringing six kids out wit ya on a
day trip wit out losin' yer marbles.

Jacinta:
Ah leave it out Sharon,
I'm sick of dat bleedin' sun.
Jerry insisted on buying all new
garden furniture plus a barbeque
and a blow up feckin' swimming pool.
Which **I** had to queue up

outside Aldi at 7a.m. in the morning.
Sher you'd think they were
givin' them away for free.
Now there's a hosepipe ban,
so I suppose that bleedin'
pool will never be used.

Sharon:
Ah for gods sake would you
ever stop with your moaning,
sure there's always a positive side
if you look for it. You won't need to
book a holiday in the sun. I always
envied you Jacinta, with your
luxury five star holidays. It's
alright for some, me and my
family can only afford a caravan
in Courtown for two weeks.
So if your back garden is crying
out for fun, me and the kids could
come over tomorrow. Wait till I
tell the kids they're going to be
swimming in your pool all day.
Sure I'll bring some burgers, sausages,
and maybe a few bottles of beer.
To hell with the hosepipe ban.
Sure if we all come to your house,
won't we be saving water, hahahaha!

Later

Jacinta:
Please Jerro. I've said Sharon
and the kids could come over tomorrow.

It's only for one day. What harm
could they do in just one day?

Jerry:
What harm could they do?
You've a very short memory.
Remember last Christmas?
And that was only for a few hours!
Absolutely not, no No NO!

Jacinta:
So that was it. Jerro said No.
What am I going to tell Sharon,
my best friend since my school days?

Next morning

Radio:
Good morning, this is Radio Dublin
with the early morning news
and weather forecast.

Jacinta:
Oh God, please say rain, i'm begging you.

Radio:
And that is the end of the early morning news.

Jacinta:
Ok, get bleedin' on wit it!

Radio:
And here is the weather forecast for
today. Widespread rain and thunderstorms

are forecast for the next couple of days.
You would be advised to keep all
garden furniture and barbecues' etc…
inside or tied down as high winds
are also forecast.

Jacinta: (singing)
It's raining men!
Hallelujah, it's raining men!
Amen!

Streets with No Pity
By Helen Sullivan

Should you visit the streets of pain, beware
Of the despair that clings to the air
It hangs from vines then drips onto the side-walks
and fills the pavement with tormented lost souls
Misery sends its whispery strands
To snare and hold you as it demands
Then coils and entwines you in its bands
As you walk along its poisoned glands
See the old women, ragged and worn
That sit wrapped in torn blankets,
Their faces crusty and grey
From a life of violation
And a world that's betrayed
See the Junkies, unaware they are lost
As they rock back and forth
Arms bare and riddled with holes
That can't disguise
The signs of their early demise
Young boys and young girls
Dart through the dim shadows
Abandoned and left alone
As they search for a place to call their own
Winos and beggars' sad bedfellows
Wander down where the mud flows
But business is slow, and the euros are low
And they end up there till the cocks' crow
The gutters are filled with the homeless
The worthless and the friendless
Each have a story, but who is willing to hear
Of those that live in Dublin's fair city
On the heartless streets held with no pity

St. Michan's Mummy
By Helen Sullivan

One day, Miss Reilly, a sixth-year primary teacher removed a small faded, brown book from her bag, and placed it on her desk. There was nothing remarkable about the little brown book, except, that it looked notably out of place, sat next to her neatly arranged textbooks and markers. The book drew several puzzled glances and one of her pupils seated in the front row, pointed to the book and asked, 'what's that?'

'My great grandmother's diary,' replied Miss Reilly who then picked up the book, that, up until the previous week had lain nestled between the rafters in the attic of her father's childhood home. At this point, her pupils became curious as to why she had brought it to school, and the same pupil called out, 'what's written in the diary?'

Hearing this, Miss Reilly cast a wistful glance at the book and replied, 'it tells of a courageous and bold rescue during the Easter Rising.'

Her answer brought about a buzz of excitement to the classroom and made Miss Reilly smile. She had intended to read from it during their history lesson on the Irish War of Independence, that afternoon. But after much pleading from her pupils to hear the tale of bravery. Miss Reilly sat back in her chair and waited for the low buzz of whispering to stop - before she carefully opened the pages that had become yellowed with time and began to read out loud.

May 10th, 1916

Easter week had seen a week-long of heavy fighting which brought about the death of many. My husband Jamie, a volunteer with the Irish Citizen Army had been assigned to the four courts. After the G.P.O fell, Pearse and Connolly fled to a house on Moore Street. But when the British began slaughtering innocents, it gave rise to Pearse and Connelly laying down their arms - which then led to Pearse penning a letter to the rest of the leaders to cease fighting.

At first, I did not believe the word on the street. However, it was while I was helping Father Michael take care of the wounded – that I discovered that the news was true. It was on the sixth day of the rising that I witnessed with my own eyes, the said paper in question being delivered to Father Michael - whom Pearse had chosen to be the bearer of his decree.

At the time of the delivery I had been attending to a young boy, and the discharge of Pearse's order brought about a lightness of the head that almost overcame me. My feet became unsteady and I found my hand fastening itself onto the young boy's arm.

I'm sure, the tightness of my grip inflicted more suffering to the lad than the wound itself, which, thankfully had not been serious, as the bullet had only grazed his flesh. Anyway, the young boy let out a yell and not knowing what else to do - I quickly let go of his arm and sat down. But, no sooner had my bum hit the ground than I stood back up again.

Back and forth from pillar to post I walked, questioning what I should do. My Jamie's end was near, and a clock with a very loud tick had begun its count down inside my head.

Time stood still when it became clear to me that I would soon become a widow – which, caused me to look around. The room was no different than what it had been for the last three days. It was filled with wounded men, women and children and those that had passed away, were placed to one side awaiting their removal. But that day, the room was different, it was the day I paid heed to the lamenting wails of sorrowful women, which I realised, had drowned out the sounds of the city.

The rat-tat-tat of machine-guns and the loud booms that were destroying our town, had become Dublin's new voice – and it was a voice that impregnated deep into one's soul. At the same time, it had also been the voice of my Jamie and the brave men he stood beside. It was then that I knew I was not yet ready to become one of those mournful women. I was not prepared to live a life of regret - by allowing my husband to die at the gallows or at the hand of a firing squad. The clock may have begun to tick but as far I was concerned - the hour had not yet been struck.

I returned to changing bandages and went about the task with no thought for the men and boys I nursed – my attention was now on saving Jamie. And by the time I had washed the blood from my hands - I had a plan in mind.

However, my plan depended on Father Michael agreeing to delay delivering Pearse's document. So, I asked the good Father to hold off with his duty, and then quickly went on to tell him the reason and of my plan.

At first, he did not respond, and I feared I would have to repeat myself, but then, the good Father looked at me and took my hand.

'Mrs Reilly, what you propose to do is a foolhardy endeavour, but it is nevertheless a fearless and brave act. However, it is a task that will take two to pull off and it would be cowardly of myself and the Lord not be by your side,' was Father Michael's answer to me. Relief flooded my bones and gave wings to my feet as I headed back to my home across from Father Matthew's Hall.

It was a home I had not set foot in since we gave it up for the cause. But that day I needed to return, as my house backed onto Stirrup Lane, and up until Thursday, the lane had been heavily barricaded with carts from the coach-house - and it was a cart that I had gone back for.

As I searched through the rubble the lane was unnaturally quiet. There was an absence of gunfire, and the silence was so unnerving that it caused the breath to lodge in my chest. A mere whisper of air escaping from my mouth brought fear to my body. However, God Almighty answered my prayers and provided me with a cart that was road worthy.

Before I made my way to St Michan's church, where I had arranged to meet Father Michael. I placed two sacks of coal, a black dress and a shawl in the cart and concealed them under a large canvas cover. We had thought it best not to be seen together, which was the reason why I had to move the cart on my own. Father Michael had been worried that I would struggle to get it over the rock and debris that was now scattered across the street. And were it not for the fact that my determination to free Jamie gave me the strength of a hundred men - he may well have had cause to worry.

My heart raced beneath my coat, as I took hold and clung onto the handlebars and pushed the cart down the road. Within minutes, my breathing became laboured. So tight did I grip those handles, that the skin on my knuckles became stretched to the point of splitting. And when tiny slivers of wood broke away and embedded themselves into the bare skin of my hand - I dared not stop and nor did I until I reached St Michan's.

Once there, I headed to the vaults below, where Father Michael was waiting. He was stood administering a blessing over the coffin he had chosen and did not turn as I drew near.

But I could see his face was pale and haggard beneath the gaslight he had lit above it, and I knew, agreeing to help me was partially to blame. He was a man of the cloth and he was about to disturb the dead. A holy sacrilege for a normal person to commit, but for Father Michael I was sure that upon his death he would be going straight into the fires of hell. And I imagined, that death was within hours for the both of us.

This thought saddened me, more so because I am no grave robber. Yet, it was I that had come up with the plan to disrespect the holy place. As I stood there waiting for Father Michael to finish with his blessing - a dreadful worrying overcame me, and I began to ask myself.

'What if the ghastly deed of ours unleashed the man's spirit.' The very notion of me being haunted for whatever time I had left on this earth was so terrifying, that I almost got cold feet.

And as I wrestled with my fears the face of my Jamie flashed before me. It was the Lord telling me, that if Father Michael could go against his Holy vows - then I could accept living with an angry spirit. Nevertheless, I was grateful when Father Michael was done with his blessing, which, prevented any further pondering on angry spirits.

The mummified body from the crypt, had been the third stage of my plan. Earlier, Father Michael had successfully carried out stage two, and got a message to Jamie explaining what was about to unfold. We removed the mummy from its resting place and dressed it in the clothes - before we perched it between the bags of coal on the cart and pulled the shawl low over its face. With little over an hour until Father Michael had to deliver Pearse's order, it was time for the final stage.

Reinforcements were due to arrive for the handover and we quickly pushed the cart up Chancery Street, where we were stopped by soldiers and questioned as to where we were going. Father Michael told them he was early for his arranged meeting with their officer in charge, and as he was a messenger of the Lord. It was his duty to help me get my sick mother to her house on Capel Street.

The soldiers drew back at the mention of an ailment but followed us from a short distance behind. I could feel their eyes bore into our backs as we turned onto Chancery Place. I was on edge, whereas, Father Michael appeared to be as cool as a cucumber.

As planned, we stopped and placed the cart facing the entrance to the courts. Immediately - a soldier shouted. 'keep moving.'

'The elderly lady has taken a spell of fainting,' Father Michael called back. It was at this point that the soldiers became suspicious and shouts of 'halt' rang through the air. We stood still and raised our hands above our head while the soldiers with their rifles at the ready, slowly advanced towards us.

I nodded to Father Michael, indicating it was time, and I grabbed hold of the mummy. Where I preceded to run as fast as I could to the Liffey and then tipped it over the wall into the water. While most of the soldiers had given chase, the ones that remained placed Father Michael up against the wall. It was what we had hoped would happen, and for the short time their attention had been on us - Jamie and six others managed to slip away. But the British didn't know this and nor did I at the time, because the butt of a rifle had cracked down on the back of my skull.

When I awoke, I found I had been taken to Richmond Barracks, where I was held until my trial. Father Michael feigned innocence to the act, and as several freedom fighters remained in the courts, they believed him. He was allowed come to visit me, on the pretence of getting me to repent for my sin, and it was he, that smuggled this diary and pencil to me. He then told me that the soldiers had combed the cold, dark waters and were livid, when they discovered it was a mummy. To save face the British never reported the incident. And that was why, behind closed doors I was charged and sentenced to six months in prison. They told me, my offence which went undocumented – was for drowning a dead body.

At this, Miss Reilly's class burst into laughter as she closed the diary. They had been quiet during the reading - but now, Miss Reilly found herself hit with a wave of questions – questions, she could not answer. For Miss Reilly had never met the brave and courageous woman who had taken part in Ireland's fight for Independence and who had been prepared to die for the man she loved.

And as her pupils left for lunch. Miss Reilly clutched the little diary to her breast and said, 'hello great gran,' to the women who had passed long before she had been born and who she had always longed to meet - and now felt she finally had.

Cracked Marbles
By Jacqueline Ross

No matter how beautiful or perfect a person or a thing appears there is always a hidden flaw vice versa with ugliness, the most deformed faces have some beauty e.g.; clear sparkling eyes, a lovely smile, thick glossy hair, great character. My Mother was convinced she was perfect, in her mind she did no wrong, so when you voiced an opinion that differed, it was received as a great insult, and there was hell to pay. "How dare you'" "who do you think you are' none of us were allowed to think for ourselves to have hobbies, to have fun, "what have you got to smile about'," get that stupid grin off your face'. Our house was not a happy one, constant bickering between children, the most common phrase "get your head out of the way, I can't see the Telly'. Cold and damp even in the summer, the Sun's rays did not extend to the windows, the house was always in shade. Food was another great disappointment, no such thing as a nice dinner, lumpy potatoes and greasy mince slammed on the table in front of you, if you were lucky, some days nothing. One dinnertime we complained about barley in the stew so the next time she put lots more in with larger lumps of carrot and big strips of onion. It was not like a scene from Oliver, no matter how hungry, you never asked for more, instead grabbed some bread and jam and ran for the door before she could catch you.

The women that lived on our street looked old to me, dry and wrinkled, worn out from the inside because of the daily hardships they had to endure; many never lost their spirit and were good-hearted kind people. Sometimes you would hear a laugh when a group of women gathered and I would wonder at the transformation taking place as they smiled. My mother never stood and chatted with these women she thought she was above everyone and walked around with her head held high. I grew up surrounded by interesting characters in a large Housing Estate on the North-side of Dublin, the largest in Dublin at the time, crowded with young children. Our street was like a little town, impossible to keep secrets. If you saw one of your friends rushing and asked where they were going they usually replied' I have to go on a message for Mammy' The children were like little postal workers, delivering secret little notes on scrappy pieces of paper to houses, 'My mammy said could you lend her any spare potatoes until tomorrow", "my mammy said have you got a spare onion", "Could you lend mammy 2 shillings until Friday', no shame in this as long as you kept your word and repaid the debt. there were people who could never pay you back, but that was left unspoken, it was charity, some people had a soft heart and did not like to see children go hungry, they gave something, if they had anything to spare, most times clothes were too worn out to be given away. We lived at the top end of a long road, people had to pass our house to get any place, the bus into town, food from the corner shop, the Health Clinic. From the age of nine I was the babysitter to my five siblings so had to spend a lot of time indoors I was a lonely child maybe that was one of the reasons I became a people watcher, standing at the little window at the bottom of the stairs hidden by a tall statue of the Pope I am sure some people noticed and this caused me great humiliation, I could sense their pity. I created a fantasy life around the comings and goings of the people passing by. The weekends were the best. Saturday evenings some couples went out for a few drinks together, all dressed up to the nines. Suits and dresses collected from the dry cleaners that day, the men, hair slicked back with gel, shirts ironed and starched proud to be seen with a good looking wife holding onto their arm, dying for a perfectly pulled pint of Guinness, the women wearing high heels, lip stick and powder, smug and happy to have such a decent loving husband, looking forward to their three or four pink Babyshams. Children soaked in the bath, given their treats for the night Pink Lemonade, Swiss Roll a packet of Wine Gums for each child, Saturday was the best day of the week, sticky toffee apples were sold around the doors. All children looked forward to this treat, it was devastating to take a bite only to discover an old apple with brown spots, no crunch, soft slippery syrup that slid off to stain your face no matter how wide you extended your jaw, with great pride we displayed this red stickiness on the tip of our nose, chin and cheeks, the first bite the messiest, you had to study the apple and bite at an angel. lucky children were given money to go to the pictures, children grilled each other "has your Mam got her rollers in', *"Hurray they are going out '*, some grew excited thinking what new pranks they could pull on the babysitter as they liked tormenting them. A break for everyone. My mother was too mean to pay a babysitter, so there was never a break in our house I was the babysitter from the early age of ten. My father played golf on most weekends so my mother would arrange to meet him at the pub, I was given chores and warnings before she went on her merry way. I am sure I gave my siblings a tough time as I was not mature enough to cope. Another good time to stand watch was the hourly mass times on Sunday mornings, some families went together, sometimes women alone as their husbands were sleeping off the hangover and would attend later. If you noticed a woman walking too quickly her head scarf pulled around her face and head down you knew she probably had a black eye or some mark on her face, these women were never brought out. She would rush to the church before her neighbours to sit in a dim secluded corner or behind a pillar away from anyone she knew, ready to disappear like a puff of smoke.

Mrs Moloy, her face covered in a thick layer of Ponds Cold Crème, rollers in her hair always ready to go somewhere but where could she go, no such thing as women drivers in them days, the men would be shamed if they allowed their wife any freedom outside of the home, Of course a lot of women ran the house with an iron fist but that was not spoken about. Mrs Murry would not allow her children to play with us as our family of seven children were an unruly lot, so she confined her children indoors, on their way to and fro to their car they kept their eyes averted so they did not have to say hello, she had her husband plant large thick hedging back and front so that in a few short years you could only hear muffled voices, silhouettes coming and going. The hedge grew quickly, became so high_that only a tall adult could peek over. This hedge cut them off from the rest of the road, I imagine they thought they lived in a stately home with its own grounds. I must admit I was envious of their daughter Jeanie, we were the same age, but different in most ways, she was a proper little lady, always dressed so well, not a hair out of place, freshly ironed clothes, she also had the one possession I longed for, her own bedroom, I could only imagine what that would be like, a place you could go to read a book, draw or paint, lie on a clean bed, daydream, if you chose to, away from the constant squabbling, lock the door and feel safe for a while. Seven children in two bedrooms, I shared a box room with two bed-wetting younger sisters so it was not a pleasant place, no peace ever, this made me an angry child who would not obey rules, especially if they did not make sense. One day in school I was called to the front of the class to be humiliated and terrorised by the School Inspector, he warned I would be sent to a Children's Home because I mitched from school, I laughed at him and told him to just try. I will never forget the shock on his tight mean looking face, a child had dared to brazenly ridicule him' he who instilled fear by his very title' in front of the teacher. I knew my Father would not let this happen, if I was dirty, or had no homework done I went to the field and sat under a tree for the day usually I had a story book to read. I found myself a lot of times flowing upstream going against the grain did not follow the heard. There is usually a reason for acting and doing things a certain way. I choose to stay out on the house as much as possible. My friends and I had great times playing on the street. Whatever happened on the street was never as bad as what happened indoors. I was very capable of looking after myself, I could stand up to any bully, I usually answered with a clever witticism whenever anyone called me names, over the years I developed a thick skin and most insults bounced right off, this skill I learned the hard way taught to me by both of my parents. I refused to become a crybaby.

Our other close neighbour was a woman called Mrs Connel, she liked to know what was going on so spent most of the day in her garden or on the path sweeping, morning noon and night, she was a nasty piece of work and hated to hear children laugh it really upset her, actually sent her into a rage, when she spoke her false teeth took on a life off their own, spittle flew from her mouth, her venomous words chocking and leaving her gasping for air I gaped at her in bewilderment not understanding why she was so upset all the time, as well as a cruel demeanour she was not blessed with good looks and closely resembled a witch from a Grimm fairy tale with her course grey hair and deep set eyes, she would sometimes carry a bucket of dirty water to throw on the path so my friends and I could not play hopscotch, occasionally we got wet, we still giggled, I think from shock, She spoke with a high pitched shriek, I never heard her speak in a normal voice. If I got lippy with her she would bend down to my face so I could see the madness behind her eyes, threatening to tell my father, and she would, this lack of respect and poor attitude of mine enraged her for some reason. I honestly did not know why, was I supposed to respect her, to fear her, to honour her, for her brutality, harshness and spite, just because she was an adult. I would watch from the window as she waylaid him as he got out of his car, god knows what she was telling him, I could feel the muscles in my stomach tense, the longer she spoke the more I dreaded the reaction of my father, if he was in a foul mood he would not listen to my version of the event I would get a slap, or a rap on the head, and a verbal assault which was much worse and which went on for a long time, I was very young maybe 8/9 years old at this time, feeling devastated inside, a slow death by many cuts, the ground falling away until you were in a dark void, trying not to show the pain caused to your soul. She and my mother did not see eye to eye, if there had been a disagreement_she would act with devilment, and stop my father on his way in from work have a bit of fun flirting with him, This drove my mother crazy I knew there would be a row so I skedaddled out of there quick as I could, I watched as she laughed and joked and threw her head back as if she was a pretty young woman, Father was a very handsome man my mother was jealous of any woman who spoke to him, Dad was sometimes flattered by this attention other times annoyed as all he wanted was to sit down and eat his dinner.

There were many fine days growing up in Coolock, but sometimes the bad memories overshadow the good. You had to learn quickly how to avoid certain people some of whom were nasty bullies. A group of us children stuck together, we forged a strong bond, understood each other without speaking of the bad things out loud. Mary with her thick wild red hair and face covered in large brown freckles had to be home every evening by seven her parents were strict and her father smoked a lot of woodbines. Ann with her protruding top teeth which caused a lisp, her parents could not afford braces, her father had a metal plate in his head, so people were extra careful when he was around, Dolores super brainy and quiet, she usually organised ideas of what to play, petite and had to wear large heavy glasses which made her eyes seem nearly as big as her head, she had no need for them when playing out in the sunshine, but her mother made her wear them at all times, so when we were out of sight of her house she took them off and carried them very carefully terrified someone would break them. I am sure to outsiders we resembled some of the convent girls that could be seen from time to time in the inner city, with our skinny frames and pale faces, the clothes we wore looking faded and past their sell by date. Playing outside was a time where you could turn your back on your worries, live for the moment, no troubles to worry you. Concentrate on the game at hand be it Marbles, one of my favourite games, the colours beautiful like rare gems. Burrowing your hand into a bag of marbles, feeling the smooth cool glass run through your fingers was comforting. Skipping with long ropes that stretched from one side of the road to the other, this was hard work five or six of us skipping, Piggy, the smell of floor or shoe polish wafting from the tin, jumping onto numbered squares a race to finish first. Swinging on a thick rope around a lamppost, sometimes your friend would push too hard and cause you to painfully body slam like a starfish into the pole, this started many rows. The best days were the ones spent playing in the fields away from prying eyes. If you were very lucky, spotting a Rabbit bobbing in the tall grass, a Red Squirrel running swiftly up a tree. Collecting Bee's in a glass jar, always letting them go as soon as the competition was over. Standing well back as the bees were usually angry at that point. Climbing trees, daring each other to climb higher and higher, collecting pretty daisies to pull the petals off "he loves me, he loves me not' to braiding hairbands, bracelets, The beauty of old gnarled trees with thick branches draped with a chunky frayed rope with a splintered piece of wood utilised as a seat. Swinging out in a wide arc across a narrow stream hoping not to fall off, leading a posse of small children to collect crab apples or blackberries, denying the pain of scratched hands and arms, having wild adventures, your mind could take you to great places if you let it. Sometimes we thought we were the famous five, or Little Women acting out scenes from stories read in an Enid Blyton book.

Of course all good things come to an end, One day we were told there was a group of builders putting up a wall to the entrance to the field and ran like the wind to see what was happening The Government rezoned the land at the bottom of our road to build factories as far as the eye could see, not even a patch of grass was left. Builders blocked off the road with a very high cinder block wall. The top was smeared with a thick black gooey tar like substance to deter climbers. Us children were in shock at this monstrosity, in mourning for our beloved playground. Reflecting back it was a blessing to have this treasure for a few short years.

Soul Mate
By Jacqueline Ross

Jules heard Harold Whistle as he closed the front door, his outside face firmly in place. She was sitting in front of the mirror examining her face before applying makeup, the large bruise underneath her left eye had slowly turned from a deep purple to a jaundiced yellow, had she enough concealer, sometimes she needed to apply a couple of thick layers if the bruising was pretty bad, of course she could not leave the house if the swelling was at its height, she just looked disfigured so she stayed indoors, ordering shopping online, missing work was the big worry, and this had come to the attention of her boss, she had missed attending the signing of big money contracts lately and was on the cusp of being fired, and she needed her salary as Howard was very tight with money. Sometimes Howard hit her where nobody could see, blows to the top of the arms or kicks to the stomach and legs. These injuries were painful to be sure but they could be easily hidden. Her Mother would turn in her grave, most of all she missed visiting her dad, making up excuses,' Sorry Dad cannot visit you this week, I have a bad cold, chest infection or earache', the earache was true as she was sometimes left in a lot of pain from her head slamming against the wall, her father would suggest she go to the doctors,' You must be run down pet' If he ever found out the truth it would kill him.

Tonight was their fifth anniversary. Jules had planned to cook a delicious dinner for Howard. Her menu for tonight's meal was a starter of fresh oysters, followed by steamed Halibut, asparagus and buttered baby potatoes which were a pain in the arse to peel, but she knew what price she would pay if Howard was displeased She picked up her large wide-brimmed hat, her special sunglasses with the large frames and rose to face the day

She had begun the day with a trip to the farmers Market in Howth, it was not an easy place to get to 2 buses forward and 2 back. But that was the price you paid to source good quality fresh food, expensive but what the hell, Halibut was Howard's favourite fish'. While she was there

Jules decided to buy a bucket of scrap fish to feed the Seals in the Harbour, it gave her time to rest and clear her head, it also lifted her spirit to see the antics of the large Seals with their beautiful trusting brown eyes. If only she could take the form of one of these great beasts and swim away.

Jules returned home to set up the scene for a romantic dinner, using her best glassware and crockery, starched linen napkins, scented candles that the makers hinted could vamp up male desire, It came 7 o'clock Howard should be home, Jules started to fret the dinner would be ruined, She declined to ring him, as he said this amounted to control and nagging. At 20 past 7 Howard shuffles down the hall shrugging off his suit jacket, pulling roughly at his tie, his shoulders slumped and looking grumpy, Jules frequently tried very hard to bolster his mood, but tonight she decided to let the full bodied red wine and good food mellow him.

Jules smiled proudly as she served Howard his meal. Eventually she sat down to eat and watched as Howard carefully examined his Oysters as If she had laid a trap and was trying to poison him. She sat looking at him marvelling at his ability to shovel so much food into his mouth, he had only taken one forkful when he dived again to slurp up more, not looking or paying attention to what he was eating, he was such a pig, his cheeks bulging with food. He even resembled a hairy piglet with his shiny pink face and beady eyes. There is an old saying "You cannot make a silk purse out of a sows ear." How true. Cracking under the strain of being polite her smile frozen in place. Her head started spinning with questions, Why am I with this man, We have nothing in common, for God's sake he has no opinions or interests outside of himself, no manners to speak of, moody unpredictable very disrespectful, A totally different man to whom I fell in Love with, there is an Irish saying Street Angel and House Devil, this was very true of Howard, People outside the home thought he was funny and generous, great craic, but the opposite was true. After very little conversation he stood and declared he was going to watch some shite on the TV.

Jules sat at the table looking at the mess of congealed food, the discarded Oyster shells, is this what will become of me, hollowed out discarded; this is not the life I had imagined. This constant effort to please Howard, everything for Howard, what about me, I quietly slipped off my shoes I rose from the table and went into the lounge where Howard was slumped in front of the TV, she shouted FIRE FIRE, Harold jumped up in fright I lunged for him and gave him a swift powerful kick to the chest, Harold collapsed back into the folds of the couch stunned, eyes glazed gasping for breath, he was dead in thirty seconds, watching him struggle was the most fun Jules had ever had with him, she would have liked to use a longer form of torture to give back some of the pain she had endured but it was important to her not to get caught, She had the rest of her life to live, otherwise all her planning and research would be in vain. YouTube is a great asset she had researched Martial Arts on a second hand laptop in various hotspots around Dublin and practised in the house every time she was alone. You can learn how to do anything if you set your mind to it and once you practise, put the work in you will get the results you want, and she very much wanted this result. Jules calmly looked around took a deep breath and prepared to seem distraught whilst on the phone to emergency services as she knew these calls were recorded. She recalled memories of her dog Bruno who had died of old age to get her in the right frame of mind. Fingers crossed all will go well; His death certainly looks like a Heart Attack and who would ever suspect the meek and unassuming Jules of carrying out such a vicious attack against her Soul Mate. When it comes down to it, bullies beware as you never know when the tide will turn against you and you become the target.

Joe Cotter was born 22nd November 1960 in Palmerstown. He attended St Johns College Ballyfermot for second level education. He received a Diploma in Legal Studies from Rathmines College of Commerce and worked for 27 years in administration for Dublin Corporation (Dublin City Council).

He presents a weekly Country Music programme on TogetherFM community radio and is a member of the Peoples College Drama Group.

He also writes a monthly Pet Owners Corner column for Palmerstown News and has had articles published in Pioneer magazine and Alive paper.

He has been writing poetry, short stories and playlets since 1980s, and was a contributor to the **Ballyer is 70** book.

He hopes to publish a book of poems in 2019.

When he's not working abroad he lives in Palmerstown with Carmel, Cormac and an Irish setter, Rusty.

Adam's Apple
By Joe Cotter

I was one of four in my cluster in the orchard. I grew wholesome and red under the gaze of my God. In the mornings the misty dew of night fell from me and I glowed radiant by the caress of warming sunshine. I didn't care for my siblings on my tree. They were misshapen and pitted with weeping lesions. I however, was round and wholesome as a special apple should be. I was the blessed one; the beautiful one; the perfect one of my breed.

God decided I would be his temptress to his upright creatures. My perfect shape, my beautiful skin, my hint of luscious juice, the anticipation of my sweetness ensured I was irresistible to these creatures.

The creatures were told not to eat any fruit from my tree. This was a test. The man creature was afraid. He didn't know what this was about and he was cautious. He knew his creator only for a very short time and didn't want to upset him. He didn't eat any fruit from my tree and advised the woman to do likewise.

The woman was more adventurous than the man and had tried several other things in their world to gather information and learn. She ignored the new order. There was only one apple on the tree worth her investigation, me.

She plucked me out from the cluster of my sibling sick fruit. She felt my weight, admired my handsome figure and my perfect skin. Turning to the man creature she said "see no need to be afraid" and she bit into my body. The pain was unbearable. I was rendered bleeding to my core. My juices ran like molten streams of lava and I burned. The woman gave my body to the man and he took a bite. It didn't matter now I had been made so perfect and so beautiful.

The man looked at the woman and tossed my carcass to the ground.

A Ticket to Ride
By Joe Cotter

A half- eaten Crunchy bar's crumbs covering
mother's guardian angel prayer, stained
by a leaking biro this pocket held
two years ago last September.
A scrunched up note of warning from Eileen
next door; Fido barked all day today.
Mumbled grumblings' half blister of codeine
pounding criticisms to close on dust.
A grubby Luas ticket to ride
To Infinity and beyond; a film we saw together
one Saturday afternoon at the Square.
And then I found the debris of our romance
In the other pocket of my life;
An unused johnny of despair in bed with
~~my~~ two years ago appointment card for
the VD clinic at the Mater Hospital.

Cherry Blossoms
By Joe Cotter

No cheerful cherry blossoms,
No dashing dancing daffodils,
No fruity fragrances of Fall.
No right, no wrong just fear
Last day of November.

Nineteen today and gone
Already lived too long.

No treasured girl to brighten dreams,
No fun filled fumblings to recall,
No longing lips in lust for love.
What's right, what's wrong just fear
Last day of November.

Nineteen today and gone
Already lived too long.

We laughed, we joined in
Friends brigade from school.
Their trick, we'd never fail our mates,
run away and hide from our fates.
Not right, but wrong with fear
Last day of November.

Nineteen today lost and gone
I'd already lived too long.

Copenhagen Calling
By Joe Cotter

I've had some interesting journeys in my time; a trip to Kerry with my mate Dermot in 1979 in an Anglia which took 5 days, 2 breakdowns and 1 engine change, cycling around Messina in Sicily during a refuse collectors strike where no rules of the road apply, a day in JFK airport New York when I hadn't enough dollars left to even buy a McDonalds and 2 days in 1985 in Istanbul being followed by scary looking men in dresses rank as trips worthy of recall. However, my trip to Copenhagen in March 2017 is the most memorable of all. It proved to be the most ironically comical, the most frustrating to endure and hopefully a never to be repeated journey.

A long weekend in Copenhagen was planned by Carmel and I for March with direct Ryanair flights at very reasonable cost and accommodation centre city. We were to travel out on Friday morning and return Monday afternoon. All systems go we would be travelling the following week.

I had applied online for a temporary position in the Civil Service and had been selected for interview. I expected to be called within a few weeks. The Sunday before our trip to Copenhagen I was called for my interview by email and text. I was to attend on the following Saturday morning which was bang smack in the middle of our Copenhagen weekend. I thought I'd stay at home, go for my interview and Carmel could go to Copenhagen as planned without me. I reckoned she'd enjoy the trip and maybe even more without me. Not so; she asked me to find a flight online to get me to Copenhagen to join her and we'd both come home with Ryanair on Monday.

I found a flight on Norwegian Air - Dublin to Oslo with a connecting flight with them to Copenhagen but it wasn't until Sunday morning. I'd get into Copenhagen on Sunday afternoon and enjoy the remaining part of the day sightseeing, have dinner and a few drinks. We would have a few hours on Monday morning before flying home Monday evening.

You know the saying "the best laid plans of mice and men oft go astray"? Well that was me sad to say.

Carmel flew out on Friday morning; I brought her to the airport and was back home at 9 o'clock to have my breakfast. I walked the dog, brought the old dears to the parish centre for their dinner, did some writing and prepared for my interview.

I spoke with Carmel who said Copenhagen was beautiful and wished me luck for Saturday morning. I refrained from going to the pub as my interview time was 8.45am and I didn't want to be bleary eyed. The interview went well and I was promised someone would contact me about a contract. I was pleased. The dog minder came to collect Rusty for boarding and I had the remainder of the day to myself. Going for a walk, reading, some writing and evening service followed by dinner occupied my time. I of course called Carmel and said everything was on track for the following day. Against my better judgement and a nagging conscience I went to the pub. I felt a celebratory drink with a few mates was in order.

I imbibed heartedly in the pub, enjoyed the company and the music on the jukebox and arrived back home at around 2am. My flight was at 8am and so I knew I had plenty of time even though I hadn't a bag packed or made my packed breakfast for the plane.

I woke at 5.30 and was not firing on all cylinders. I had difficulty packing my few pieces and getting myself ready. My tummy was somersaulting and my head was both fuzzy and headachey. However, I got to Dublin airport in sufficient time for my flight. Of course, I hadn't made the packed breakfast but I bought some on the plane.

With a flight at 8am, arrival in Oslo at 11am and a connecting flight from a different terminal at 12 noon I was anxious when we didn't leave Dublin until 8.30 but the stewardess assured me I would make the connecting flight okay. I settled in my seat and had a snooze for an hour or so. We landed in Oslo at 10.50 and I was delighted I had an extra 10 minutes. But then I forgot where I was going to and so instead of changing terminals and looking for my flight to Copenhagen I ended up at a gate where the Stockholm flight had closed. Sugar, maybe I could still get on the flight if I bypassed the gate and headed for the plane. I made my way through the walkway and came to the door of a plane. "How did you get here?" asked an air steward. I ignored his question and asked if this was the plane for Stockholm. "No," he replied "we've just de-planed from Kiev. And how did you get out as far as here?" I scarpered as fast as I could and back into the airport as I was sure security would be interested in me now.

Back in the airport it suddenly occurred to me I should have being travelling to Copenhagen; we'd been in Stockholm the previous year. And so I looked at a flight information screen and started to run; my flight was leaving in 5 minutes. This time when I got to the correct gate with no Norwegian Air personnel behind the desk a burly security guard wouldn't let me go any further. No use pleading my case; I was snookered. I made my way to the Norwegian Air information desk in the main concourse; of course there was no staff member there. In utter frustration and near despair I phoned Carmel in Copenhagen and I wasn't a happy camper. I complained bitterly about the short transit time I had from one flight to the next omitting I had made a huge blunder myself. We decided if I was able to catch a flight to Copenhagen that afternoon I should continue my journey. I was a bit unsure and said I'd be better off going home maybe.

No person came to man the Norwegian Air desk and so I decided to try my hand at the Lufthansa information where a woman of around my own age was sitting at the desk. I think she may have questioned my sanity when I greeted her with are you certain I'm in Oslo and not Frankfurt or Düsseldorf or wherever. Yes, she told me, you are in Oslo airport and how can I help you?

Me: I've missed my connecting flight to Copenhagen. I'm tired and frustrated and would like to get out of here.

Helga: Where do you want to go to?

Me: Out of here anyway to anywhere.

Helga: Copenhagen?

Me: Maybe Dublin

Helga: Let me have a look at that for you

Some minutes later Helga informed me I could catch a Lufthansa flight to Gatwick, London with an Aer Lingus flight from there to Dublin.

Me: How much does that cost?

Helga: Lufthansa Oslo to Gatwick 210 euros and Aer Lingus Gatwick to Dublin 390 euros

Me: No way am I paying that money, especially as the shortest part from London to Dublin with my national airline is nearly twice the cost of here to London

Helga: How about Copenhagen then?

Me: Alright see what's it costs

After a few minutes Helga came back with her answer

Helga: 108 euros for a flight at 17.05 this evening arriving in Copenhagen at 18.50

Me: I'll take that so

Helga: And you'll be able to have a lovely romantic dinner with your wife in wonderful Copenhagen tonight

Me: Yes that would be nice

Onwards and upwards I thought to myself as I made my way to the check in desk for my flight to Copenhagen. I informed Carmel I'd be with her around 7.30pm. She had told me it was a 20 minute transfer from the airport to the station after the central metro station where she would meet me. I had a lovely flight to Copenhagen and although the stewardesses were jovial and good natured. I didn't trouble them much save for a German sausage roll and water. I arrived safely and on time in Copenhagen airport.

From my research I knew that it cost 3 euros 60 cents for the metro ticket into the city and I duly bought my ticket from a machine. I searched the overhead information screens and found line 4 which was for the central station. I duly trotted off to the platform where I awaited the arrival of the train. I got on happily anticipating meeting Carmel in 20 minutes time. I looked at the map of the line which was over all the carriage doors. Grand three stops to central station. Perfect. We arrived at the central station and I imagined I'd be at the next station within minutes. But the train didn't stop at the next station or the one after and then we went over ground. I was beginning to panic. I found out through sign language and some choice Anglo-Saxon words by me that this was a mainline train bound for Germany and the very next station was the last for 100kms. I decided to disembark at the next station. I phoned Carmel as soon as I was on the platform.

Carmel: Where are you? I was expecting you a half hour ago

Me: I'm in some God forsaken place at least 30 miles from the city and I'm very pissed off. Why in the name of God did I say I'd come here. I'd love to be at home now phoning you instead of in this hellhole of a place.

Carmel: Okay, okay; take it easy. Will you be able to get a train back do you think?

Me: I suppose I can but feck this is absolute shite

Carmel: Make sure to get on a train coming back to Copenhagen

Me: Do you think I'm a right eejit altogether? Don't answer that; I know I am

Carmel: See what you can do and let me know when you're on your way

There were 6 different train tracks running through the station. I had got off onto the most right platform. No ticket office was open so I decided I'd take my chances and hoped no ticket inspector boarded my train. There were 2 train tracks in the middle and so I moseyed over to them and selected the one whose information monitor told me directed me towards the city. To be sure though I asked a family of 2 adults and 2 kids; thankfully they had English and the man informed me I was right about the direction but only 2 trains a day on that line stopped at the central station in Copenhagen and he advised me to go to the platform furthest away from the one I had disembarked on.

Grand I was sorted at long last and phoned Carmel to say I was waiting to board a train bound for the central station due in 3 minutes and would see her very shortly there. No problem. Apart from being nervous about having no ticket I was amazed to find whole families getting on the train with their bikes and plenty of bike racks to store them. In a short time I was getting off the train and making my way through the central station. I rang Carmel to see where she was waiting for me.

Carmel: When you come as far as the McDonalds you should see me

Me: I can't see a McDonalds.

Carmel: As soon as you come up on the escalator from the underground you'll see it straight in front of you

Me: What escalator? I wasn't on any escalator

Carmel: What can you see from where you are?

Me: Listen I'm going outside and we'll get a landmark to meet outside

And I exited the station. When I left the station I stood a good bit back and discovered the outside of the station was very similar to Kingsbridge railway station in Dublin and I said so to Carmel. She was mystified as she couldn't figure out why all she could see was a square new style building with no stylish façade. Again we started on what we were able to see in the vicinity. Using her google map on her mobile she discovered that Copenhagen had 2 central stations; one for the metro underground and one for the mainline trains. She asked me the names of nearby streets and with me in constant contact with her I came to a street corner she could see on the map.

Carmel: Walk up that street, go past the station again and continue straight on until you come to Grand Plaza. I'm walking towards you and I'm very close to our hotel.

Joe: That's great; at long last I'll be able to get a drink and calm down

And so we met in down-town Copenhagen. I was so relieved to have finally arrived I threw my arms around Carmel and said never again let me travel on my own anywhere by plane or train.

Wonderful, wonderful Copenhagen and it lived up to all my expectations of the city.

Gilbert Shakespeare, William Shakespeare's Brother
By Joe Cotter

Gill Shakespeare here, christened Gilbert and I'm William Shakespeare's younger brother. I don't seem to have any other purpose in life anymore other than being his brother. He's two years older than me and is a gigantic pain in the butt. He wasn't always though. When we were small we were the best of mates ready day or night for adventures; robbing orchards, snaring rabbits, tormenting the little pigtailed girls and swimming in the Avon river.

We went to the priest's house in Stratford for schooling. I reckon it was that fool of a man that made a scribbler out of Will. He kept praising him for every poem he composed and every story he wrote and by the way those stories were often mine. I was a good storyteller. I still am but the written word is the in thing now. Some of my stories he made into great plays and poems. Romeo and Juliet, they were Rob Young and his girlfriend June Sutherland. King Lear was Malcolm Smith who had three good for nothing daughters and no sons. He died in misery, haunted by their greedy and nasty ways. Yes I learned how to read and write and do my sums. I became a haberdasher, able to cut cloth to measurements, weigh out nails and spikes, gauge how much wool I can get from a sheep or how many planks a builder needs to lay a floor or build a privy. It's a real job not like plying your words for pay.

I've been lucky, built up a good business in London and came back to Stratford and opened my shop. A lot of Will's time is in that Globe Theatre place he runs. I supplied wood, furniture, curtain drapes, lighting and all; in fact nearly everything the builder needed. He stills owes me for the stuff and I've been waiting three years for payment. It's a tidy amount in fact.

It's not like he can't afford to pay me. He gets £10 for every play, £10 for every book of poems and £100 annually for being poet in residence to the Queen. Oh, he's a courtesan now and parades about like a peacock. His clothes are of the highest quality and he wears a disgusting amount of jewellery. He lives like royalty. I pity his poor wife Ann. He's making a fool out of her by strutting his stuff in court with the ladies in waiting and bedding young serving maids every night. Pity his looks are spoiled by his baldy head. He'd nearly be as handsome as me but for that shiny tonsure.

Last year I got really cheesed off about the money he owed me and filed a suit to have it paid. The court case was held here in Stratford last November 2nd when Magistrate Buckle held the winter sessions. I made a good case to have my money paid right away to me but Magistrate Buckle ruled that as Will's income was irregular and not guaranteed I was to be repaid by instalments of £10 on the first day of each season. I'll probably have all my money by the time I kick the bucket. Judas Priest that's justice for you in 16th century England.

These days the other scribbler Ben Jonson and Will seem to be stealing each other's ideas and characters. They're supposed to be in competition and have big public rows. I've noticed though some story or fellow Ben has in a play turns up in a play or poem by Will later on and vice-versa. Their public spats are just a sham. They're as thick as thieves sharing their ideas and such.

William has found his scribbler brother in Ben Jonson. I hope Will's a better brother to Ben than he's been to me.

Post Script

Gilbert Shakespeare, William Shakespeare's younger brother was born in 1566. On the election of their father, John as Alderman, both brothers availed of the free education their father's position had assured them. Gilbert became a haberdasher and followed his brother to London about 1584 and opened a shop there. The brothers were frequent visitors home to Stratford and eventually Gilbert moved home and opened a shop in the town. He never married. In 1604 he appeared in Stratford Court in connection with a lawsuit; the details of which are not now known. He died at the age of 46 in 1612.

Salvation
By Joe Cotter

I looked for freedom and found futility,
I sought solace and got only sorrow.
I wished for wisdom and gained witlessness,
I found fervour but lost my serenity.
I wanted help but would not listen,
I was invincible and lost my humility.
I despaired and prayed out loud to God
And at due time He answered me
Seek help and believe you are my son.

I surrendered and I won my freedom,
I listened and I learned to live.
I give and gracious wealth is given me,
I am mere sponge on loan from God
I have a debt of gratitude to pay.
I love and I seek no recompense,
I thank my Lord for He is good to me.

Kasey Shelley is a writer and poet from Dublin. She has been performing in the Irish spoken word scene for two years. Her poems touch on love, heartbreak, mental health and being a woman. She has been published in Flare and Harness magazine as well as the Selfies & Portraits anthology. She is behind the scenes of open mics, The Circle Sessions and Dolcáin's Cellar. She is currently working on her first poetry book and novel (if she can stop procrastinating!). Her Facebook and Instagram pages are Kasey's Scribbles.

A Storm is coming
By Kasey Shelley

The hard rain soaked through her cardigan, seeping into her skin. She stood on the corner, asking herself what to do next. She cursed herself for not grabbing her phone. "You didn't have time to grab your coat Maggie, never mind the mobile!" She reasoned. She wondered if he'd be asleep soon. The last whiskey taking effect. Perhaps the surge of adrenaline would keep him up. Waiting.

"You should have just kept a closer eye on the pork!" She muttered under her breath. She thought of going to Jo's. It was only a thirty minute walk but she couldn't handle the 'I told you so' right now. Jo never said it but she could always tell what her big sister was thinking. Besides, she'd make her stay the night, which brought its own problems. Maggie had no uniform for work which meant coming home in the morning. The hangovers were worse than the night before. He hated Jo, and he knew that's where she would have been. Knew that was the only place she could have gone.

Maggie caught the eye of a woman at the bus stop but quickly looked away. She knew she must have looked mad. The woman wore a pant suit, her giant umbrella shielding her perfectly preened hair. Was she going home to shouting? Maybe she wasn't married. A woman all about her career. No one to report to each night. Maggie dreamed of that life for almost ten years now. No dinners to be made. No sour taste of whiskey on top of her in the mornings. Being able to stretch out in bed. Suppose she could do that the nights he didn't come home. Why did she stay? She stopped asking that a long time ago.

The wind had begun to choke her. She could feel the stares from the passing traffic. It was time to go home. She walked back the ten blocks, her shoes squelching. Half way, she passed their local park. It was small, only one set of swings for the children. She smiled to herself as she thought of the many Sunday afternoons they spent here. She would make a nice picnic for them. He would read the paper out loud while his head rested in her lap. She loved listening, running her fingers through his hair. My God he had a beautiful head of hair. Jet black. Once upon a time.

She stood at the park gate, looking at the beginning of the storm's results. Rubbish was strewn everywhere, the swings going wild. A thick branch, about two feet long, broken clean off a tree had landed by the gate. Bushes were almost pulled up from the root. Chaos. She carried on. No point in delaying the inevitable. She trudged those five blocks, fighting the gale with all her might. Children were pointing from the cars now. She didn't care. Just get home.

She barely had the door open when she heard the chair drag along the floor. She ran up the stairs. "Where the hell have you been?" The slurring began, rising in volume. "I'm getting my uniform and going to Jo's. Do not try to stop me." Her voice trembled from the bedroom. "Oh no you're not. I don't want that bitch knowing our business." The stomping started on the stairs. As his foot reached the last step, she swung the branch as hard as she could. He stumbled for a second, his hand reaching out. With two loud bangs he fell back, landing awkwardly near the bottom.

"Frank?" She called over the bannister. Nothing. He didn't stir. She stood there, the branch still in her hand, shaking. "I...I told you not to stop me..."

After Eight
By Kasey Shelley

She tapped her nails on the table, glancing at her watch. The restaurant began filling quickly. The band was setting up. She put her hand up as the waiter tried to approach her again. He scurried past, dropping the menu like a ninja. A menu. Did he think she was here alone? That she was stood up? Not this time. He promised her he'd be here. That he was finally going to tell his wife. She grabbed her coat and stormed out.

It only took her fifteen minutes to get to his front door. She peered in the kitchen window to see if he was home. That's when she saw him. His hands, placing the chain around her neck. His lips, a kiss on her cheek. She screamed. They both jumped, looking out at her, terrified. He ran to the door but she ran on to the road. Wheels screeched. He held her close, called for help. Begging her to hold on for him. She smiled as her eyes closed one last time.

She tapped her nails on the table, glancing at her watch.

Island of the Dolls
By Kasey Shelley

He only takes the normal girls. The plain ones, ugly you could say. He makes us pretty though.

He takes us in the dark of night or in a quiet park perhaps. That's when our journey starts. The island is beautiful, remote. One way on or off; his boat. We go to his workshop.

He examines us, our flaws. Our potential. He chooses our new clothes. Pretty cotton and lace dresses with bright colours. He styles our hair. Pigtails, maybe curls. Then the exciting part. His eyes light up as he begins. Drawing on freckles, rouge on our cheeks. A little lippy, but never too much.

Then we meet the others. All so pretty. Drinking tea, playing in the garden, cooking. We were brought from all over. Galway, Athlone, Kerry and even Dublin. A new one comes every week.

In fact here he comes with a new doll to play with now.

Perks of the Job
By Kasey Shelley

My boyfriend Roger got me a job in the company where he works. Don't worry we won't be working together; he actually just got a promotion. He's on the road a lot while I'm in the office. It's a pretty sweet deal I get a free laptop and phone; they just take a small contribution out of my wages each month.

I was looking through my new laptop and came across some photos. Someone must have had it before me. I couldn't help but browse. Some were work photos, holiday snaps, dark ones I couldn't make out. And. Is that a body? I flicked to the next one and gasped. I slammed it shut.

I asked Rachel in IT do they recycle laptops. "Yeah, when someone leaves the company or upgrades" I was debating showing the photos to the police but wanted to have a name. I asked who owned the laptop before me. "Oh what a coincidence. Roger did."

Wanted: A Victim
By Kasey Shelley

There were three knocks on the door. Loud but slow, hesitant. Jeremy ran to open it. Disappointed to find a young woman standing there.
"May I help you?"
"Em..." She mumbled, clutching her book bag that looked huge around her petite frame. "I'm Jordan..we spoke-"
"Jordan? Sorry this must be a misunderstanding, you're a –"
"A girl."
Her long blonde hair framed her rather plain face. "Well, yes. I was under the impression from your emails you were a guy."
"Your ad said you were looking for a male. I knew if I said I was a girl you wouldn't reply. May I come in?"
Jeremy looked beyond her, to see if any of his neighbours were about. He moved to the side and she brushed past him. The scent of strawberries followed.
"You have a lovely home." She went straight towards the book shelf. Her fingers ran across the spines. He watched her in silence. "Voltaire. This is a first edition?" Her eyes lit up.
Jeremy smiled. "Is that a question or statement?"
She giggled. "Sorry I'm a bit of a book worm." She put the book back in its place.
"Look I think there may be some confusion. In my ad I was looking to-"

"To kill someone." She said casually as she picked up trinkets on the mantelpiece. "Me." She looked around and laughed at Jeremy's horrified face. "We've been emailing for two weeks about it. About when, how..." She moved towards him.
"Yes. Well I thought you were a man."
"Does that matter?"
"Yes."
"Why?"
"How old are you?"

"19."

"I think you should go."

"Why?"

"This was a mistake. A joke." He forced a laugh. He walked towards the door opening it. She stood still in the middle of the living room, dropping her bag with a thud. "Please, you should go."

"No. We both know what you wanted to do tonight. Just because I don't have a penis shouldn't matter. Unless.. that's what you're into?"

"No!"

"Then it shouldn't matter that I'm a girl. You want this. And so do I."

"You're just a kid. Why-"

"Because I don't wanna be here anymore." She looked down to the floor. "And I can't do it myself."

"Is this a set up?"

"No." She looked up at him, hopeful.

"You should go." He gestured out the open door.

"It can be." She didn't move.

"What?"

"We had a plan. I have transcripts. Of you describing in detail what you were going to do to me. The cable ties so I couldn't stop you once fight or flight set in. The points you would hit with your knife to cause a quick death. What you wanted to do with my body after. The cutting. Exploring. Learning."

"Listen –"

"No you listen. We had a plan. And if you don't go ahead with it just because I have tits then the first place I go after here is to the police."

Jeremy laughed "And what? Tell them you want to die? They'll lock you up in psych."

"No. Tell them I spend my free time trying to catch perverts on Craigslist and that I stumbled upon your ad. And went along with it to catch you out. There are cyber vigilantes all over the net. I'd be just another one."

"You fucking bitch."

"Yes. And I'm a determined one. So either a, you can get arrested, or b, you can kill me so I don't leave here and rat on you. And if you're doing b, you might as well go ahead with the plan."

They stood in silence for a moment, staring each other down. Jeremy cracked first and slammed the door. She smiled.

"Wonderful." She went to her bag and pulled out a bottle of wine. "I guessed you were a red guy, was I right?"

Jeremy sighed. "You're crazy." He went to the kitchen and got two glasses. She followed him in.

"That's what they say." She poured as he checked all the blinds were down and the back door was locked. "I do have one extra request." She handed a glass to him.

"Oh yeah, what's that?" He took a gulp.

"I'm a virgin."

He choked on his second gulp, red dripping down his chin. "What?"

"I'm a virgin. And I've made my peace with dying. I don't want to live in this world anymore. I don't want to suffer. But I can't make peace with not experiencing one of the most fundamental aspects of human nature. So..."

"Are you kidding? You want me to fuck you before forcing me to kill you?"

"Firstly I'm not forcing you to do anything. I gave you two options. And is the thought of having sex with me really that repulsive?" She folded her arms uncomfortably, giving her small breasts the illusion of being full. He looked at her. She wasn't ugly. Just not attractive. Her hair was a boring shade of blonde. She wasn't a girl who would stand out.

"I just don't think it's a good idea mixing business with.."

"Pleasure?" She picked up her glass, inhaling. "I'm not frigid. I know how to please a man. I just haven't had the opportunity. I can assure you it would be memorable." She leaned in and kissed his neck softly. She put her hand down to his pants. "Your body is already agreeing with me."

He gulped back the rest of the wine and moved past her. Pouring a second glass, he nodded. "OK, fine. Fucking Craigslist man."

She took the bottle and sat down on the couch. "Come. We can start once we finish the rest."

"First lesson in being sexy for a man, don't tell him what to do." Jeremy sat next to her, sipping. She lifted her leg on to his lap, her dress revealing her porcelain thigh.

"So, why did you place the ad?"

"I've had thoughts for a long time. They've become more frequent lately."

"Have you ever?"

"Some animals. It was never enough. Why did you answer the ad?"

"You made an interesting proposition."

"You know what I mean. Why do you want to die?"

"The world is a horrible place. It's hard to see past the darkness." She placed her glass on the coffee table.

"What about your family, friends?"

"This isn't a therapy session." She stood up and began unbuttoning her dress. It fell to the floor, revealing her equally plain body. She climbed on to his lap, her small frame seeming too heavy on him. She started to undo his belt. He moved his hands to stop her but realised they weren't moving. Her body started to wave in front of him. His head fell back. She grabbed him by the jaw to make him look straight ahead.

"First lesson in being a killer, don't post a fucking ad. A lion doesn't plant himself in the middle of the herd and expect to be successful."

"What?" He slurred, his eyes falling on the coffee table to her full glass of wine. "You psycho bitch." His head fell back.

"That's what they say." She stood up, putting her dress back on. She felt for a pulse. Nothing. Grabbing his hair she cut a tuft of it and put in a small plastic bag. She poured the remainder of the wine down the sink and put the bottle and glass in her book bag. She headed to the door then stopped. She walked to the bookshelf and grabbed the Voltaire placing it in her bag. As she closed the door behind her she met a couple on the road walking their Collie. "Good evening." She smiled at them both. "Oh, good evening." They chimed back. When she got home she took out the plastic bag. She pulled an A4 hardback from under her bed. Flipping through dozens of pages to the next blank one, she taped the hair to it.

"Welcome to the six o clock news. A 30 year old man, who had been found dead in his home two weeks ago, was poisoned. Jeremy Dalton had been discovered by colleagues who grew concerned when he had not shown up to work for three days. Police are exploring all lines of investigation. Some of the man's neighbours said they came upon a woman leaving his home on the day he was last seen alive but have not been able to give an accurate description of her. 'She was young, blonde, and thin. We didn't really notice her until she spoke to us. We paid no mind until after Jeremy had been found. She wasn't very memorable, you know.' There were no other witnesses and police continue to investigate but the case seems to be hitting a dead end."

Why Did Yas Leave?
By Kasey Shelley

Screeching tyres, graffiti on the wall
Racism, sexism and just good old fashioned bullying
The gangs who were like cliques, are you in?
Or are you out?
The address on a CV, the bus to a different school
The paedophile down the road, the rapist next door
The junkie across the way and the gangster next to her
The girl punched in the face because
Scum and violence don't discriminate
The 'RATS OUT' to the twelve year old
Simply walking by
The flames from my Mam's car
Visible from the kitchen window
The knife held up to my Dad's neck
When he tried to stop it
The life that would have almost certainly
Only gone one way

Maria Francis is a graduate of Trinity College Dublin, where she studied, Drama Studies &The History of Art and Architecture. Maria is an ardent advocate of Theatre and film, and likes to dapple with the pen. As Edward Bulwer-Lytton wrote in 1839 in his historical play Cardinal Richelieu "The pen is mightier than the sword"

Ambient Static
By Maria Francis

A crescent moon
A stolen glance
The belated dawning of desire
Awakens from its slumbering terrain
Eclipsing the contours from, the circumference within
Recollections dissipate
Scatter to the four, corners of imagination
Distant suns calibrate
Merge into the myriad
Streams of consciousness
By chance to dream
The dream of righteousness
Whispers anew, prevail through
The punctured wounds of apathy and regret
Beguiling the stars from their celestial constellations
As we patiently fall between the cracks
The pinpoint shards of light
Reflect and refract across the illusion of illicit motion
The shedding of bone and skin
As the perennial pursuit of enlightenment passively begins

Maria Francis

Pacific Daylight Designs
By Maria Francis

The eternal hope of spring
Eases gracefully into, a myriad existence
The palest light gathers
Beyond the perimeter walls
Illuminating the path of least resistance
Hands entwined
Descending slowly to the sacred stones beneath
Held in silent prayer
Renewing the essence of the symbolically righteous beliefs
The shifting sands of summer
Segway mercifully to the expanding consciousness
Evolving through a precious, patchwork of dreams
As the darkened forest brightens
To a chorus of joyful requests
Hearts beguiled
A carnival of tranquillity
That's so eloquently regales
Protected by the incandescent elements
As the ancient words of wisdom conspire to consistently prevail.

Maria Francis

The Urn
By Maria Francis

How much I asked in a loud voice. How much for the Urn, I held tightly against my chest, for fear someone else might take it from me. No response from the dark-haired man behind the makeshift barrier, a plank resting on two chairs. At last he turned to give me his attention. He looked at me, as if he could see right into my soul. He took a step back, as he asked what it is you want. How much do you want for the Urn I asked? He replied, give me a tenner and it's yours. I could see the uncomfortableness in his eyes, he wanted rid of me. Not taking my eyes off him, just for the pure fact that I was making him uneasy. I agreed to give him the tenner. As he put his hand out to take the tenner, I held onto it, it forced him to raise his head and look into my eyes, I looked back at him and with a smirk on my lips, I let the tenner go and said thank you. As I walked away, I could feel his eyes burning into my back, I could tell he too had dark secrets.

As I walked along the avenue where I lived carrying the Urn against my chest, I began to feel a certain comfort in the Urn, and the Urn in me. I turned the key and entered the house, put the Urn down, on the kitchen table, lifted up the lid only to find it had the ashes of a body in it. "I knew it, you were sent to me" I began to rub my hand up and down its cold porcelain, as I did so, I said welcome to my home, or should I say, your new home.

Over time I began to have conversations with the Urn, asking all kinds of questions. Who are you, where did you come from, how long were they living in the Urn, and why? I started to call it Ashie. I would sit there every evening talking to Ashie telling him all about my day. Then I mistakenly told him my darkest secrets. Unlike all the other men from my past, Ashie was a good listener, and he cunningly bullied me into revealing things that should have remained hidden forever. It began innocently enough, with the exchanging of favourite holidays and pastimes. But before I was even aware of the shift in mood, he'd steered the conversation into much darker territories. He proudly admitted to having beaten up his best friend for having an affair with his wife, and then casually enquired as to whether I'd ever found myself in a situation where I'd resorted to violence to achieve justice. He was obviously pandering to my vanity, and it worked, because I was so thrilled that he'd confided so candidly in me, that I felt compelled to reciprocate. Revealing something as important as this was never going to be easy, so at first, I was quite hesitant and uncomfortable with my delivery. But, as I eased myself into the process, I found my true voice, and the floodgates opened in a torrent of words. I excitedly explained how I'd tracked down and murdered the man who'd raped and brutalized my younger sister. He'd only spent a derisory two years in prison, while she was sentenced to a life of depression that eventually led to suicide.

At her sparsely attended funeral, I vowed to exact revenge on him, no matter what the consequences would be for me personally. I had no idea whether or not I was even capable of taking another human beings' life, but when I eventually confronted him, and he showed absolutely no remorse for his crimes, I had no hesitation in plunging the knife into his corrupt heart. The expression of horrified surprise on his face as he lay dying in the gutter, is a memory that I shall treasure for the rest of my days. Perhaps God's sense of decency and justice prevailed, for the knock on the door from the police that I kept expecting, never materialized.

Still the whole episode had taken its toll on me emotionally, causing many a sleepless night, so it felt reassuringly cathartic to finally be able to unburden myself by discussing it with Ashie. Initially he was extremely sympathetic, and understanding of my situation, but it didn't take long for his true motivation to rise to the surface. Blackmail was too sordid a word for him, to actually use, but the implication was that unless I acquiesced to his wishes, then he would be forced to resort to it. So, I'm currently sitting in my car, preparing to drive to an address, where a widow, and her late husband's best friend reside together. With a gun in my pocket containing two bullets, and instructions on how to implement his nefarious plans. He's left no stone unturned, and he has repeatedly choreographed me through every minute detail, for he has faith in no one's abilities, except his own. Perhaps he'll be satisfied after I've successfully completed the task but I seriously doubt it. For the list of people who have angered him is extensive and his pathological thirst for revenge is unquenchable.

Marad Frantas

My Cliff Richard Rose Bush
By Margaret McDermott

My Garden was my favourite place to spend my spare time. I would spend long summers weeding, plucking and shovelling my way through the dense playground that was my garden. Weed, weed, pluck, pluck, shovel, shovel. That was the tune to my gardening that my ears loved to hear.

During the summer of 2015 my garden had grown particularly wild, so much so that I decided to employ a gardener to maintain and nurture it. So I flicked through the local advertisements in search of my new Gardener.

After a week of searching I finally found my new Gardener. His name was John Rose and by God could he shovel. He could dig his way out of a tunnel and he'd still be amazing. He was the best Gardener/shoveller I'd seen yet. And I'd seen a few in my time. And the Rose Garden, my goodness could he look after my Rose Garden, under one condition that he didn't touch my Cliff Richard rose brush.

I'd spent many a long day looking after my Cliff Richard Rose Bush. It wasn't until that sunny weekend in July 2015 that John set a foot wrong. I sauntered into the Garden ready to water the Rose Bush when I saw John, weeding, plucking and what looked to be pulling at my beloved Cliff Richard Rose Brush.

"Away from my Cliff Richard Rose Bush at once!", I shouted. "But I was only looking after-" Before he could finish his sentence I reached for the shovel and hit him over the head. "I found a perfectly nice place for you Mister John Rose." I buried his dead weightful body in the lovely Rose Garden. The roses grew up through the garden but it didn't make me feel any better.

The Meeting With Acupuncturist Lily Silver Balls
By Margaret McDermott

Mel had an appointment with the one and only Lily Silver Balls. She was named this due to the extraordinary amount of balls she could juggle in her hands at any one given time. My my, she had an eye for ball juggling like no one else I'd seen before or since.

Mel was a modern day gravedigger so he would spend many a day digging for those graves. Dig dig... clunk clunk... would be his mantra. So as one can imagine he needed his back to be taken care of, pronto!

He had heard many stories about the wonders of Lily Silver Balls, but nothing could prepare him for what he was about to find.

The day was here, the appointment booked and all ready for Lily and her magical wonders, Mel set off in the quest for the wonders of her skills huh huh!

An Asian lady, what looked to be Filipino answered the door to him. "How can I help you?" she asked as she greeted him with a friendly smile. "I am going to be performing acupuncture on you today."

As he lay himself down on the bed, his head lay rested between the hole in the bed. He sensed something wasn't right but he proceeded to carry on. "Ok Mister Mel, I'll start with the needles now."

"Just put the tip in until I see if I like it," he said to the acupuncturist.

As the needles kept jamming in his back a big merciful whack hit his face. "What was that?" he said. He awoke to a massive humongous pair of silver balls dangling in front of his face.

"Oh so that's why they call you Lily Silver Balls!"

"That's right, it must be a Ladyboy!"

True Power
By Margaret McDermott

It was the winter in Toronto and one of the coldest the city had seen in the last fifty years, but Betty was going to get her hands on Wayne Blakefield no matter what it took. She had spent many years pining over Mr Blakefield and nothing was going to keep her from getting her little mitts on him and his wondrous talents. He had over fifteen number one hits under his belt during his chequered career and one stood out the most in Betty's mind. "POP GOES MY HEART!!!" was the tune she cherished very dearly from her teenage years. They would have put Spandau Ballet to shame.

So when she heard Mr Blakefield was coming to Toronto ahead of Valentines Day to do a press conference for his upcoming Greatest Hits album and tour, she hopped on the bandwagon and thought to herself that this would be the perfect opportunity for her to snatch Mister Blakefield away and serenade him on her upcoming birthday, which would be Valentines Day, February 14th.

Her plan was in place so she went through her checklist.

Her car was filled with petrol – Check

The snow and frost had been cleared from her wind-shield – Check

Rope, handcuffs, black masking tape – Check

Thick white cloth, chloroform and pliers – Check.

Checklist completed, so off she went.

Mr Blakefield had planned to hold a press conference in the Toronto Convention centre in Union Square that very day, so Betty set off on her way and headed towards the convention centre. She pulled up outside to a line of waiting photographers and news reporters. What is this, she thought. so she skipped the queue of photographers and headed through the side entrance of the centre.

When she arrived into the big hall. the room was set up and the stage ready to present Mr Blakefield to the crowds of adoring bloodthirsty fans. Her plan was in place, so she made her way to Mr Blakefields dressing room in anticipation for his arrival and subsequent kidnapping by her dear self.

She made her way towards Mr Blakefields dressing room. She brought along with her, her holdall bag filled to the brim with all the essential tools she needed for the grand kidnapping. A rat-tat-tat she knocked on the door.

"Who is it? Come in!" the person answered in a rather odd voice. "It's me Mister Blakefield, Betty O'Neill, your biggest fan!"

"I was wondering would you be as kind as to sign my autograph book I have of you."

"Come in and close the door after you," the person answered.

"Hello Mr Blakefield, I'm so happy to meet you." Betty said as she reached out to greet him with a handshake. "So pleased to meet you," he said, as she shook what seemed to be a handful of razor sharp manicured acrylic nails. Something doesn't seem quite right, she thought, but she proceeded to carry on. He wore a pale blue silk Japanese dressing robe.

"I'm just going to change into something a bit more comfortable dahling!" he said, as Betty waited at the dressing table. "Your voice sounds a bit different from what I remember Mr Blakefield, rather high pitched," Betty announced. "What do you mean my dahling? It sounds rather the same to me." "Okay, if you say so," she replied agreeably.

While getting changed Mr Blakefield fumbled around behind the dressing screen.

"I'm just going to get these knockers in order and pop on some tights," he said.

"What do you mean your knockers and tights?"

"Well these adoring fans won't wait for my wonderful drag act forever."

Mad Alice In Wonderland
By Margaret McDermott

"I want to break free, I want to break free." Alice said to the Cheshire Cat, as he gave her the biggest grin she'd ever seen with his full set of pearly whites. "What do you mean you want to break free, my dear Alice?" "I mean I want to break free from this Wonderland and return back to my homeland of England."

"The Queen is rather mean and wouldn't share a single bean, not even with Jack and the Beanstalk." "I mean this Wench just sits on her gold bench and passes out orders like we're a crackpot bunch of Northerners."

"Oh Alice cut the Queen some slack and get off her back, you know she likes an old front, back, crack and all over body wax."

A Poem On Winter
By Margaret McDermott

As snow comes falling down
I sit there with a frown
But wait, what is the matter
For sure I hear the sound
Of little tiny pitter patter

Much to my surprise
The snow is in demise
For when Winter comes
We know we'll have so much fun

Back to the little tiny pitter patter
Sure it's only Julio and his little French bulldog Snatcher
But you were meant to be here yesterday
Oh no need to worry
I have gone and made us
A lovely chicken Thai green curry.

The wise old woman of Omni Centre
By Mary Oyediran

She waddled and shuffled like a penguin, she carried her burdens on her chubby wrinkled hands, clutching two heavy looking crumbled plastic bags on each hand.

As I walked out of the Omni shopping Centre in Santry in Dublin, I couldn't help but observe this old lady needed a helping hand.

Living in the city capital of Dublin, the citizens have taught me the religious significance of doing" a good deed for the day."

As a benefactor of many good deeds from total strangers since I arrived in Ireland in 2005, I was constantly on the lookout for an opportunity to be "of good cheer." Do good at least once a day!

Impressed and convinced that one good deed deserves another and love makes good vibrant communities. I was moved to take action as often as possible.

As she waltzed slowly ahead of me, her whimsy, thin grey hair held by black lace band in small bun, piled on top of er round pinkish head marked her for attention.

I couldn't see her face, but her plump pear shape body with straight trunk legs riddled with swollen veins resembled a railway track, no stockings, laid bare for all to see.

"She has painful varicose veins "I muttered under my breath.
She needs help! She was struggling to balance those bags!

The superwoman in me was awakened, ready to rescue a senior citizen in distress. To perform the arduous task of relieving her weak muscles of the heavy load.

These happy thoughts brought joy to my heart.
I felt great inside of my soul.
"My good deed for today!"
If pride was a precious pearl necklace, I was wearing it!
Funny, nobody else seems to notice her!

This must be God! After all, only my eyes were opened to see her needs. I have been divinely chosen! Hallelujah!
Applauding myself, I plucked up the courage to stalk her for good.
I was encouraged to pursue, then relieve her of her burden.
Quickening my pace, I caught up with her.
"Hello" I smiled broadly," Can I help you Ma'am? Trying to sound as Irish as I can.

I held out my arms towards her bags.

She stopped swiftly. Her deep green eyes smiled at me, a beautiful dimple dipped on her left cheek, brightened her heart shaped flawless rose complexion.

She must have been a beautiful damsel in her heyday. Exquisite fine line laughter lines soften her loveliness.

"Thank you my dear but I'm grand!"
She waddled on!

I felt rejected but not defeated!

Walking behind her from a safe distance, promised myself to be available in case she became exhausted.

She paused in front of the garage.

I stopped abruptly too!

Maybe this is my opportunity to assist her. She must be tried! The garage stood about 200 yards in front. The old damsel moved slowly toward the big black garbage bin located adjacent to the front of the garage.

Placing all her bags on the pavement.

She picked up one bag at a time, she emptied the content into the large rubbish bin with precision. Not a drop or dust fell to the ground.

Then, she folded each crumpled plastic bag neatly for recycling, clutching them under her wobbly jelly arms.

She continued to shuffle her feet, much faster and never looked back.

I was astounded! I chuckled!
Turned back, laughing uncontrollably.
Bystanders were watching me and smiled politely.
"She must have lost the plot." I can hear them whisper.

Today, I had gained practical insight and a valuable home economics lesson from this wise old beauty queen.
I crowned her the Queen of Thrift! Now, I know the secret of reducing the weight of my bin.

I am richer for this new knowledge. It must be applied immediately to reduce my financial burden of getting rid of waste.

Amazing, I had set my heart to be blessing her but she helped me!

I learnt three valuable lessons that will remain with me for life.

Firstly, I must never judge a person by their outward appearance!

Secondly, the older generation has acquired a wealth of applied wisdom. The younger generation must seek these practical strategies diligently from them.

Lastly, being thrifty is a life skill! It should be taught as part of the curriculum in all schools.

As a dog is never too old to learn a new trick, we must be determined to keep learning until the trumpet calls.

He Dried Up My Tears
By Mary Oyediran

He dried up my tears,
When bitterness engulfed my heart,
my soul tormented, hunted by fiery darts!
Reproach, disgrace and shame became constant companion in widowhood,
They clung to me like a knighthood,
isolated by all, choking, cracking up, complaining,
Soaked, drenched, weeping,
wailing "all is lost, all is gone"
...Suddenly I felt a gentle glow
His love surrounded me!
"Hush Hush I AM is here!
It was Jehovah Shammah - The Lord is there!

He dried up my tears
when betrayal arose!
Friends became enemies!
Families like foes!
Desertion, devastation and destruction,
Encircled by frustration!
No way to turn.
Bawling, bewailing and bemoaning
Bursting into tears in deep fear, Lamenting
"Nobody loves me.
Nobody cares"
Confused and faithless -
Struggling, distress, stress
...At once His voice came as clear as running water
"I will never leave you!"
It was Jehovah Nissi -
My BANNER!

He dried up my tears
When sickness rose
To torment my flesh
Headache, neck ache, backache
Every nerve frayed
Croaking, cackling, grumbling, grunting and groaning
The pain cleaved to like lovers now
One flesh refusing to leave.
Antibiotics, painkillers, tranquillizers, more pills
made a fertile bed in my stomach.
Disfiguring, distorting, dismantling
mind body and soul.
Laying, helplessly, muttering,
murmuring. Mumbling
"Take me home Lord, NOW!"
Curtain of my eyes shut!
Feeling like a walnut!

LAY STILL - THE FINAL CALL!
Swiftly He sent me His Word
"By my stripes you are healed!
Instantly the chains broke
I was free! Free to live!
Jehovah Rapha - my healer!

He dried up my tears,
when recession, regression
with depression came to stay, gripping my account
they nested, rested inviting
the twins Inflation and deflation
Prices rising never falling stagnation caused examination
Adding hard times multiplied by bad times equals sad times .
Now in the Red, quickly bury my head residing in bed,
everything dead! WHAT A DREAD!

Can't pay the mortgage, can't rent!
No dosh for phone, electric or gas.
How to climb this hill?
No money! No food!
Help! Is there a food bank?
Promptly I heard a whisper
"Look to me, your helper"
It is Jehovah Jirah - my provider!

Let Him dry your tears
Give Him all your fears
In Sickness He heals,
In Pain He comforts,
When rejected, He elect.
Weakness He gives Strength,
When poverty strikes, He sends riches.
In the pit? He pulls out of the ditch!
Jehovah El Shadai - Almighty God!

Nancy Dawn (real name Nancy Matchton Owens) I am the facilitator of Ballymun Library Writers and I am a writer a poet and an entertainer. The arts are what I adore and I myself am a work in progress!

A Nursery crime
By Nancy Dawn

There was a thief in the night
He was ever so sneaky and I suspect he was a professional
Did you get him on the camera
Did you report him to the authorities
Did you put him away for life
He stole my little boy you know
There is a man who comes in for a cuddle

I want to report a boy missing
Someone switched him for another one
His features are bigger
And his full heart shape lips only cause me heartbreak
It is only a matter of time before some female takes advantage

My little boy is missing
and another lies beside me sleeping
his mop of hair is thick with promise and
his long eye lashes would make a girl jealous

Somebody stole my boy I'm telling you
This one speaks with a deep timber
And his legs go on and on and I don't know what his dreams are made
of anymore
I know I sound like I am repeating myself but I would like to report a
crime

It happened really quickly
They poisoned him with a potion and his clothes don't fit him anymore

My boy is missing and this male gives me a bear hug that makes me
lose my breath

I nearly fall over but regardless he comes back for another and another
Hold on now there is something familiar here
I am ever so grateful to father time
He has given me a peep of what the future brings
It's only superficial though and thank god for that
Inside this man lives my little boy
And so my crime is solved for now

A matter of time
By Nancy Dawn

Time is a bully that controls me
starting and stopping abruptly

Time threatens my dreams of yesterday
and writes lines in my face I never asked for

Time keeps me marching
when I am weary and want to stand down

The whips and the chains of deadlines and constraints
never waver

Time is a silly face staring at me
with numbers and arrows competing for my attention

Time is a Fuhrer
delegating orders in my ear
and I must answer at some stage

Time ridicules my intentions
and makes me pay for my usage
like an electricity bill

Time makes me accountable
and robs my credibility

Time is sweet in love and hell in loss
and I never can go back

Time repeats my mistakes over and over
and lessons will not be learned.

Time is running out
tick tock tick tock
days into years
and I fail to keep track

Time is an earthly measure
a concept that I can shuffle off like an old skin

Time tortured life and I bought into it.
I don't need it in my final destination
at the end there is abundance and I can sleep forever.

The Balloon
By Nancy Dawn

He let the balloon go
the breeze brought it away
It weaved in and out of the fluffy borders
It was alone
It had no intention
It had no burden to bare
Its destination was unknown
up and up to god knows where
the yellow tear drop dissolving into the distance
freedom
heaven
oblivion

Kill the winter
By Nancy Dawn

He creeps in like a predator
Slowly but surely
A dark shadow swallows the light
Like that of a dimmer switch
Watch him as he robs the leaves of colour
 And makes the branches talk to one another aggressively
Howling like a coyote
In a language I cannot understand
A chill that turns one's head around
Jealous of the bear hibernating until springs
sleeping peacefully through the carnage
oblivious to the short daylight
A blanket of foggy grey mist covering the world
Lonely isolating feelings erupt
As claustrophobic cabin fever
Until the flower buds arrive and pop their head through
Showing a sign of life
Of continuing
Hold your breath
Until he goes away
Live among the children that play in the snow
And do snow angels
leave it for the skiers who relish in the powder
but for those of us who feel the weight of S.A.D.
Kill the winter

When The Chips Are Down
By Nancy Dawn

"I'm doing the best I can," Daniel barked down the phone. "It's not easy out there, there are many more competitors now, cut me some slack will you?" His CEO was two minutes away from letting Daniel go. Daniel back peddled as fast as he could.

Trying to compose himself he said "Just give me till next week. I'm so close to closing two accounts, please I need this."

He hated the sound of his own voice pleading.

"Okay," he said smugly "you have till the end of the month. Get your act together buddy, a little less of the sauce and you might have it." He bit his tongue and counted to ten. It had never been easy working with family.

Daniel hailed a cab and looked over his contacts in the back seat, it had been three weeks since he had really done any business. It was partly his fault he knew, he was not sleeping as well as usual and just didn't feel on top of his game. The odd cocktail of a few Irish whiskeys and Xanax were taking their toll.

As he went inside his porch he sighed, spotted three brown envelopes and as he flew inside the door he ripped them open. Two bank statements, and the electric bill. He threw his brief case on the floor and headed for the JD at the bar. Out of coke, he thought. Oh well, down the hatch anyway, he couldn't even taste it anymore. It was about getting the job done. Stopping the constant banter in his head. Pushing the anger down. He threw off his shirt and put on his tee shirt and sweats. He felt a run might help stop the jitters and when he got outside he ran hell for leather. He took a left at the stop sign and belted up the main road towards the bridge. His heart was pounding but he welcomed it. He loved the outdoors and the freedom he felt jogging, but then the thoughts came. The self doubt, childhood stuff he had never moved past. Somehow, he felt a failure. He couldn't deal with the pressure. His fiancée pushing the marriage thing and the father in law holding a business over his head like bait. The bank refusing him a loan because of an old debt. He made a decision just there and then, he was going to end it. He walked over to the railing of the bridge and looked down. It would be better for everyone, things were spiralling and they were not likely to get better. A negative train of thought. He looked down and imagined what it would feel like if he fell. He imagined the worst, failing at the attempt. He took a deep breath and climbed one leg over. He grabbed his phone and texted 'I love you Mags, but you deserve better.' He stared at it for a moment and as he threw his other leg over the railing, a young man ran to him shouting; "Don't do it, whatever it is, it's definitely not worth it!"

"How do you know?" The guy was clean shaven and had huge blue eyes that stared into space. There was a hurt Daniel couldn't help noticing as he looked closer at the man.

"Well, I don't, but I have another way."

"What do you mean another way? You don't know anything about me!"

"No, that's true but trust me I have another way."

Daniel snapped, All his frustration seemed to come to a head.

"Just get out of here."

"No," he said "I do, I have another way. I felt just like you did last week I swear, but I am better now. Look, I know this doesn't make sense, but a friend saved me."

"Saved you? Who? Jesus? Jehovah? Who? God... I've done the god thing... Please, I can't do it, just go, please!"

Daniel turned and put his leg over the rails again.

"I have a friend who can help you."

"How? What are you talkin' about?"

"He makes chips."

"Fish and bloody chips, give me a break."

"No, this guy makes them."

"What do you mean he makes chips?"

"Computer chips."

"Computer chips?"

"Yeah, he makes them and he will put one in you."

"Are you for real? What?"; Daniel screamed; "You are wasting my time. Leave me alone. Just get lost."

"I was in a bad place too honestly, they put a chip in me. I was able to stick a pin in myself and start all over. You can too."

"You are out of your friggen mind, are you? You're mad?"

"You can do this please. I felt exactly like you, only worse. Get down and follow me."

"Why should I? It's not gonna help."

"It will! Listen to me. No more baggage. Can you understand? You start over. Back to your old factory settings, just like your phone, only it's you, get me?"

"What? Not possible!"

"You will be who you were before you got messed up."

"I was always messed up."

"No, think about it?"

"I can't remember when it was okay."

"That's why you have to go back."

"You are messing with my head, I don't need this."

"No, I am not. Please just come with me."

"You're nuts!" Daniel wiped his sweat and followed the man in a daze. "He can't help me."

"Have you got any money?" the young man asked.

"Yeah, two fifties."

"That will do, let's go!" As they walked down the road Daniel looked around at his familiar neighbourhood, his secondary school and the park with the stream. He had fished and swam with his brothers for many years. He pulled out his phone and realised the text hadn't gone. He sent it. He walked another couple of yards and was beginning to get irritated.

"Where is this guy, for god sake?"

"It's coming up. He works in the bottom of the building there."

"I know that pub. There is nobody that works there."

"You will just have to trust me, Daniel."

"How the hell do you know my name?"

"Just do."

"How?"

"I drink in your local…you are there on a Sunday in the corner, mostly miserable reading a paper."

"What? I am not. What are you talking about? Screw you!"

"You just don't look happy. Follow me in here and go back by the bathrooms."

Daniel walked back and the smell of the barrels of beer and urine made him gag.

"Follow me down the stairs." He walked down two flights of rickety stairs and then again to a room with a whole bunch of computers.

A nerdy man appeared. "What do you want? Weren't you already here?"

"No it's not for me, it's for my friend here."

Daniel puts his hand out. "I need a chip."

"What kind of chip?"

"The chip. The same chip you gave this man."

"You talkin' about a reboot chip? It will cost you."

"Yeah, yeah of course….I know."

"I only have two left. How bad do you want it?" the man with the glasses asked annoyingly.

"He wants it as much as I wanted it," the young man protested. "His life is in the toilet."

"What's your name?"

"Daniel Burns. What does that matter? What's yours?"

"Wally."

"Well, it matters. I have to look you up on the computer here, see if you are eligible."

"Eligible? What kind of racket you running here!"

"The kind that everybody seems to want? This stuff is like gold dust. Everybody wants to start over. They somehow think they will take care of something they didn't do before. It's all a crock if you ask me."

"I gotta go," the young man said. "Can I leave him here with you? I'm starving. I got places to go and people to see. I can't afford one second more in here. There is so much to take care of. I got people to talk to and be with. I got my whole life ahead of me!"

The nerd turned around and shook his hand, "Yeah you go ahead. I will check out this guy, go, do, be! The world is your oyster." Daniel watched the young guys face light up.

"Jesus," he said to Wally, "I want some of that, that was me at age 22."

"You wouldn't believe that is the same guy from last week. He was homeless, shaking and using as well. I saved him."

"Not you, your chips."

"They are my chips, my invention. They are a miraculous thing. I have hit it big I'm telling you. Everybody wants what I got." He smirked and Daniel could see Wally's face clearly as he turned toward him. He could see he was small and hunched over and seemed to cave in on himself, he was so painfully thin.

"What about you? Would you not reboot yourself as well?"

"Don't need to be working on myself. I am happy out."

"But you don't have a life and you're alone back here doing this."

"This is the way I want it. Anyway, I got one chip left today. Let's see if your a candidate."

"You said two."

"I lied."

Daniel started to panic. "What do you mean if I am a candidate? Is there a chance that I might not get this today?" He took him by the scruff of the neck and held him against the wall.

"You will get it, if your eligible. Calm down!"

"Okay, what do I have to do?"

"Answer some questions, I put in your details."

"Listen! I need this, no matter what, just take the hundred and give it to me."

"You don't understand," Wally said, "you have to fulfil certain criteria."

"Yeah so you said."

"Okay your name."

"I told you, Daniel Burns."

"Age?"

"48, well tomorrow's my birthday. 49."

"Wife, fiancée, partner?"

"Fiancée, her name is Maggie. Mags, everybody calls her. What does that matter?"

"Its part of the program that determines if this will work. Occupation?"

"Account exec...Hayden industries."

"Any bank savings?"

"No nothing, tapped out."

"Not according to this."

"What? What's it say?"

"It says you got 200,000 there."

"What? Can't be!"

"Yes, you do."

"I had nothing this morning... I don't get it."

Daniel could hear his pocket vibrate... It was a text. He pulled out his phone and looked. It was from Mags and read 'Daddy transferred money to your account. Did you get it?'

He shook his head in disbelief. "This is so weird! Well, any more questions? Am I in?"

"You realise you will lose your 200,000 do you? If and when you reboot, you start again with nothing."

"Yeah, I know," he said. "Does it say I'm eligible?"

"Yes, you are."

"Great, I can't be bought anyway."

"Are you ready?"

"What?"

"Give me your arm." And as he started to push in this microchip, Daniel started to bleed a lot.

"Ow!" Daniel yelled, "That hurts!" and he jumped up in his bed and opened his eyes with a start.

His wife turned to him and put her hand on the small of his back. "Hey, you alright?"

"What a wacky dream. It was so real." - Then he repeated "reboot," over and again as he held his arm.

Maggie turned to him, "What?"

"If you could start your life all over again would you?"

"No. I don't think so.. you?"

"No not likely, I might not have met you."

"Maybe that would have been a blessing."

"What? Why? I love you, what are you talking about?"

"I mean there are no guarantees are there?" Daniel said with a smile.

"Nope. Life is a gamble," and as she reached around his waist she pulled him down to her.

"Love you."

"Yeah, ditto, goodnight."

"Night."

Natasha Helen Crudden is a punk-influenced poet, author and photographer. Her previous works include poetry collections "Barbed-Wire Cage" and "Ctrl/Alt/Delete", novel "Empire Evolution" and punk-poetry EP "Detonation Day". Her poetry and prose has been featured in several literary publications and she has performed on various platforms, including Electric Picnic. She is a regular on the Dublin open mic scene and performs at literary and arts nights throughout Ireland.

Lazarus
By Natasha Helen Crudden

I feel I should tell you,
As you don't appear to realise,
You are dead.
I killed you
With the stroke of a pen
I wrote you out of the script –
Yet here you are,
An apparition, full-bodied and corporeal,
In front of me
in the queue for Marks and Spencer.
A disconcerted Lazarus
Stealing glances back
As you recognise me,
beneath the surgeries of time,
From another life.
You rake the edits
From some stray scintilla
Of the me that you once knew -
Count the furrows in my brow,
Your eyes, the twin pools
Of want and trepidation
I recall from a past
All but forgotten,
Perched on the precipice of flight
At any sudden movement I might make
Yet simultaneously, overwhelmingly
Compelled to stay.

Luna, Eclipsed
By Natasha Helen Crudden

I rise to greet you
Before dawn
The cosmos wrapped around you
like a blanket in the early morning frost.
I see you
Blushing velvet
Peeking from your covers
And you see me,
Moon-faced,
Holographic skin
Luminescent in the darkness.
You float
In the realm of the unearthly
And I fumble with my phone
In vain attempt to capture
Some fragment of your beauty
for my own
To keep once you're gone
A token for a memory of the moment
that we shared
To hold 'til next we meet.

Noughts and Crosses
By Natasha Helen Crudden

One minute to midnight
On the doomsday clock
Becomes a ten second timer
To zero hour
An unfiltered inhalation –
The world tastes too real tonight,
Its technicolor
Too sharp

Floundering in the deep
You ink in a copybook
The mark of your salvation
And float
Nursing hatred
Clutched like a Sacred Heart medal
Itching like a fire brand
Emblazoned on the back
Of a grease charred spoon.

You begin to see it
Everywhere you look
Right angles set like razors
Into pavement blocks
Carved in the trellised panes
Of a stained-glass Brigid's Cross
You can find it anywhere
If you look hard enough
Because we want to watch the world burn
Just to see the flames.

The Carnival
By Natasha Helen Crudden

Roll up, roll up! Drive-in circus for one night only!

I grind my gears down to zero into my place, second in the queue, amidst the red and blue strobe lights enticing the world-weary traveller under the conjured canvas of the neon candy-striped tent.

At the box office, we pass the main exhibition piece; an overgrown Scaletrix run off its tracks, crumpled nose-down in the briar and barbed wire crush.

The crowd swells as the inquisitive masses of theatre fanatics are pulled toward the epicentre of the spectacle. There was no question of flogging tickets online; you can't buy this kind of publicity.

"Isn't it shocking, Patsy?" remarks one bystander to her neighbour. "A holy terror", he concurred, "and with that big funeral on as well. Couldn't be a worse night for it."

We have arrived, at the precise place, at the precise time, and we are waiting.

The expectant audience face forward, and into the ring drifts a weighty canvas of fog, whose tendrils fall away to reveal our Master of Ceremonies, Death. He strides here and there amongst the cars, allowing his presence to roll out amidst the spectators before resuming his place. With flourish and command, he sweeps an arm toward the exhibitionism of the wreckage and challenges his audience with a riddle- "How?" The riddle itself, however, is, for those of the gathering who really know, a trick- the real question is why.

The top-billed act is wheeled into the centre ring slapped on a gleaming silver stretcher, zipped up in a blue bin liner, as a dead animal caught beneath the wheels of a roving truck. We crane our necks to get a good stare at the spectacle- the act formerly known as "Alive". Our fascination with this exhibit, flung like a dead badger into a bin-truck, bubbles up to the surface the true nature of being human- our expendability.

That could be any one of us, but for the dice-roll of our Master of Ceremonies, handpicked from the crowds thronging the arena. Any one of us could be the star of this carnival of the grotesque, on our way to stratospheric fame. Hushed, we wait with bated breath, but the lead has already been chosen- nameless and faceless to us forever, but for tonight, bathed in ruby and sapphire spotlights.

With a squeak of wheels, a band of tangerine-clad acrobats whisk the second performer into the ring. The Master of Ceremonies announces the act- a tightrope-walker balancing the precarious tipping-point of the Grand Parade between life and death. We hang on our gasps, waiting for him to tremble, wobble, or topple. One foot scales the twine, in front of which is set the other. The line shakes. We sweep forward as one. Another step, followed by another and…he is over the line to the other side. With a sweeping bow, he disappears from view, to raucous applause. The Master of Ceremonies hisses. He has been cheated most grievously, and is displeased.

Molten lava splatters the tarmacadam floor like an upended paper cup of TK, flooding the banks of the white line separating the performers from their audience. The amber-coated troupe raise vermilion-soiled hands, the remains running down their costumes.

The crowd draw on heavy breath as the squalling strains of the bone-chilling orchestra screech into being. The dancers assume their positions. Their rhythms draw me in, swirling bolts of neon caught between the frantic revolutions of the performers, flashes of metal dragging briars, beats rebounding through the ground beneath our feet.

My thoughts are disconnected, whirling in the blinding frenzy of the revellers, as though under ether. We are spectators no more. The gate has been unlocked, and the performers have invited us in to share in their world- a reality existing only in the reveries of the genius- or the mad. This world belongs to us now.

The cabaret of the damned captivates, enthrals, appals and has caught me up. There is no resisting it. This is a temptation from which there is no escape.

The shades of night draw over the violet dusk, and all is transformed. The wailing symphony begins to ebb into the echoes of the hillside. The amber ensemble file obediently into their fluorescent metal tin- toy soldiers called away to serve in another epic battle.

Neon deluminates. The tent folds up its canvas and disappears into the night, leaving the fairground conjured into a misty country backwater. The circus dissolves and with it the illusion we once called truth.

The crowd holler and storm, applause flooding the gangway and seeping down the verge. We are elated. Our perception of the very fabric of the air we breathe has been irrevocably torn asunder. My fellow theatre partisans go along their way, buzzing and chattering. It's been a show to show them all, alright. Life and death and the matter of the universe have been paraded, jested, parodied and sent off stage. And we award it our highest accolade- a standing ovation in place of a guard of honour. Car doors slam. I crack up my engine. Still warm.

We depart, cramming in our heads the knowledge we have gained before we are caught red-handed and forced to return it. Knowledge- which is what, precisely? We've been served our own heads on silver platters while our decapitated dandelion remains run amok in metal cages. We are the show, and our night will come, and we will have our own audience. But what are we going to do with that knowledge? What use is it to ordinary people like us?

"Shockin' way to go, Patsy." "Ah it is, Bridie, but sure, it got us out of the house all the same."

Stopwatch
By Natasha Helen Crudden

Stop.
The clock.
Time
out.

Blinding light, burning my eyes from their sockets, pierces my head. It won't last long.

Behind the opaque fog indistinct figures weave here and there. Distantly I catch snatches of discourse in an alien tongue. My head swims as I attempt to pick out the details. My knees buckle and I faceplant cold, hard laminate. "Concentrate, concentrate!" Dr Salzar snarls from his leather-backed chair. Icy sweat pours down my brow as I climb to my feet.

"I am concentrating", I spit, barely holding back the venom I long to unleash; on Dr Salzar, on the police, on anyone who'd dare try to make me believe my brother Thomas had been murdered. Disconnected jigsaw pieces are all that remain of that night, and I'll be damned if I can manage to make them fit into a solid memory, with or without some jumped-up quack braying in my ears.

"But you were the lone witness, Kian", the good doctor presses me. "You must have seen something, heard something- even if you don't remember what it means, I can help you bring it to the fore. You do want to catch the person who murdered your brother, don't you?"

My tether snaps. "Just keep pushing, Doc, just keep pushing. You don't know when to call it quits, do you? I have no memory of Saturday night. I told the guards that, god knows I told you that over and over and still you bang me up in this fucking padded cell like some sort of demented unchainable animal, like I'm going to turn on you or myself or society at any moment. Is that what this is all about? You think I'm going cracked, is that it?"

Dr Salzar scratches his head, then leans forward on his elbows.

"We've already established you don't have amnesia, nor are you going cracked, as you so term it." The shrink adjusts his shiny Calvin Klein frames as he continues to watch me like a bug in a plastic slide. I notice the Cartier sparkle on his wrist as he drops his hand back down. "You must really rake it in, forcing people to believe they've gone round the twist", I shoot back, glossing over his observation. "Just how much did an office on the Grand Canal docks set you back, anyways?"

Salzar ignores this and continues.

"Kian, I wish we could let this go. You've suffered a terrible trauma and I wish we could leave this alone. But I've been assigned to this case by the Gardaí and they need your help to catch your brother's murderer." The quack rises from his chair, suddenly a man weighed down by years of trauma and sob stories, finally dragged to the ground by an advertising executive who refused to give in. He turns to the towering wreck of Bolands' Mill across the dock, gathers his breath, and revolves to face me once more, the shadows of his profession underlining his eyes. "Please Kian. Take me through it again."

His hand reaches for the Sony dictaphone resting on the table between us as he descends into his seat. The ruby light flickers. "Where were you on the night of Saturday the thirteenth of October, 2007?" My voice crackles and breaks. "At a party in the IFSC apartments. It was a work party, thrown by one of the senior managers- Robert Carthy- to celebrate getting a contract with a major construction company in Limerick. My brother Thomas and I had taken a company limo there-he hadn't taken Sarah with him." Salzar frowns. "You never mentioned Sarah before. Who is she?"

I straighten my slim black tie against my stiff shirt collar as I contemplate the ceiling, moulding my expression into nonchalance. "Thomas' fiancée. He brings her"- I correct myself- "he brought her to every damn corporate event to shove her in everyone's face to show just how well he was doing for himself."

Salzar observes me under his eyebrows. "Do I detect an undertone of jealousy?"

I snort in disgust. "Detect what you will, Doc", I snarl. "I'm just here to answer the goddamn questions. So do your fucking job and ask me the questions."

Salzar nods, and anchors his flimsy Bic biro woven through his thumb, index and middle fingers. "Did anything occur at this party which seemed at the time, out of the ordinary? Think hard, Kian, your recollection is clouded but clouds burn off. What happened at the party?"

I squeeze my eyes shut. Drifting fog clogs the brink of my brink of my vision as the shadowy figures weave in and about. The buzzing grows louder until it fills my ears, drowning every sane thought I have left. "Concentrate, Kian!" Salzar snaps, distantly. "The shadows are no more real than the buzzing in your brain! They are nothing more than a defence to guard you from the truth! You want to know the truth, don't you? Then pull off the disguise of the memory and uncover what really happened that night!"

I grit my teeth against his barrage of syllables, flying at me like the bullets of a firing squad.

Wish the old goat would just give up. Whatever the hell he and that red blinking light of his think they're getting out of me- "Wait."

The mist thins. Definition sharpens. Colours become discernible- reds, blues, yellows blur and merge into purples, greens and browns. Voices jabber in stereo like a rewinding tape recorder and the wavy outlines become distinct, focusing into features, faces, arms, legs, cocktail dresses, black suits, champagne flutes clutched delicately at the stems...

I swallow my rising unease. I'm in Robert Carthy's apartment, I recall, begging my rapidly-pulsing ventricles not to give away my panic. I'm in the boss's apartment, at a work party, surrounded by my colleagues, and their wives, or girlfriends, or husbands. But not Thomas' fiancée, oh no. He's swapped Sarah for the blonde floozy of the night, hanging on his arm and simpering as he cracks jokes she hasn't the cranial capacity to grasp.

I snap my eyes open. Salzar is surveying me intently. "Did", I falter, "did I say all of that out loud?" He nods. "This situation makes you angry?" A live-wire sparks in my brain.

"Of course it makes me angry!" I snarl. "We were practically engaged when Thomas managed to steal Sarah from me- and now he treats her like this- in front of everyone- without having the decency to call it a day!"

Salzar inclines his head. "What else happened that night?"
I slam my eyes shut. My colleague Scott storms over to me, eyes blazing. Scott works as research and development executive on my team, where I'm advertising executive and I'm about to cut him short on another of his damn work queries when he reaches the punch first.

"You've got to do something about that brother of yours." "I don't know what you're talking about," I retort. Scott narrows his eyes.

"Don't give me that shit, man. You'd have to be blind, deaf and dumb to overlook the fact that he's hacking our intranet and stealing our campaigns. You know what Carthy said- he's got to make lay-offs, and whoever falls behind, is left behind. Kian, we're in shit here! And if you don't do something about it", he grits his teeth as he spits out his words, "I will."

I shake my head as he disappears into the crowd. Thomas has been stealing from our team- this much I can't deny- but he's my brother, and Scott is teetering on the edge of losing it here. He's tanked enough to fuel a jumbo-jet, and if he doesn't burn it off there's no telling how far he could go.

"Tommy!" I howl as I tear through the living room, in wild search for my brother.

As I slide the balcony door open, I see him, engulfed in tobacco fumes, surveying the miry abyss of the Liffey a hundred feet below.

"Tommy." I choke on the cool night air.

"You'd better watch yourself. Scott is blitzed, and has this idea you've been stealing our ad campaigns. He's looking for a fight, Tommy, and he's serious about this. You'd better get the hell out of here right now.

My brother drags on his cigarette, and slowly exhales. "Do you honestly think I'm afraid of Scott Loughlin?" he spits. "He's going to tell Carthy on me, is he? Woop-de-fucking-do. And Carthy is supposed to believe him over me?" A figure moves from the shadows in the corner by the window. I step forward to alert Thomas, but he takes a pace toward me, a jeer etched upon his face. "Look, we all know what's going to happen. We've known ever since Carthy made that announcement, and we all decided we'd do whatever it took. It's a matter of time, brother, and your time is running out." Chips of ice danced in his pupils.

"But don't worry. Soon you'll have all the time in the world."

The figure launches itself at my brother- I am frozen where I stand, unable to intervene. Thomas chokes as his assailant plants his hands around his throat, throttling, pulverising-

My brother's feet slip upon the tiles. One final shove is enough. Something dies in his eyes as he disappears over the side of the balcony.

I turn to the reflection in the window. His face sharpens into focus- the narrow grey eyes, the slicked-back gold hair…The room swims. I lurch forward and retch. Vomit slides into a pool upon the floor. Salzar leans toward me eagerly. "Did you see him?"

I choke. "Yeah, I saw him. I saw who did it." I raise my head to face him, and a bitter smile twists itself upon my features. "Here's your fucking truth, Doc –"

"
I

t

w

a

s

m

e

!
"

Nicholas Earley

I am presently mid-way through my 72nd year on earth. My wife assures me I've been happily married for 52 of those years where we've lived in contentment in Ballyfermot, though I have to add whether our neighbours were as content is up for debate. I'll make but one claim to writing and that is that I absolutely crave it when its inspiration takes hold and my veins cannot dilate fast enough to absorb every morsel of information that's trying to grab the next available space on the page. But alas, even at my age I still lack dedication to the task at hand. Over twenty- five years ago my hearing decreased just about the time I was taking writing seriously so I don't think I can be accused of lying when I say I never did hear opportunity knocking. I've now amassed as much money from writing as my wife has from rodeo riding. To some people that situation is looked upon as failure but you see I believe they are alcoholics looking through a glass half empty.

To begin with there's no shame whatsoever in not being famous. I can walk uninterrupted down any street without any fear of being approached for my autograph and to pose for a selfie. I can shop in any charity shop and not have any fear of the paparazzi coming in and snapping me. I don't have to live in a gated community with sentries and neighbours I don't even know. And best of all I can rest easy in bed at night and know none of my family are likely targets for kidnappers and ransom demands. However, I have to say, the best endorsement I can give for writing, and mine in particular, is the sheer pleasure I derive from the laughter I create for myself. Yes, at times like that you can lock me away in solitary confinement and all I'll ask, is how long have I got. So for those who haven't got that, May the Lord have mercy on your soul. And for those who have, Welcome to The Book Club.

Are Ye Finished Digging Yet?
By Nicholas Earley

It utterly amazes me the extent some people go to defend their actions when its blatantly obvious to even a blind man that they're better off keeping their mouths shut as all they're doing is digging a hole for themselves they're never going to escape from. Better to concede defeat now than make things worse for themselves, but do they stop to think, do they ever?

Puddles opened his kitchen door and to his horror he saw his father kissing his mother-in-law passionately. (What de fuck is goin on here) he thought to himself. His father, sensing someone else in the room, turned round abruptly and said "Jazes Puddles I didn't hear ye come in, I was only givin Rosey eh friendly hug that's all." Puddles shook his head from side to side at the sheer stupidity of such a statement and replied "Is tha wha ye call eh, looks te me eh was more than friendly from where I'm standin, if ye geh me drift." Meanwhile Rosey, said to herself (He's like eh bleedin spider when he moves noh eh fuckin sound does he make.) She now took it upon herself to add her few words to the debate "It's noh what yeh think, don't be jumpin to conclusions. Yer Da was only comfortin me." Somehow or other you maybe get the idea Rosey tends to say just a bit too much at the wrong time; me too.

Puddles father and his mother-in-law could never be accused of being in the first flush of youth, or second for that matter. Rosey wasn't a day over sixty- eight (according to her anyway) and her new beau had recently blown the candles out on his sixty-ninth birthday without pausing for breath, which wasn't difficult considering there was only one candle.

Puddles couldn't hide the disgust he felt and the blatant nerve of the pair of them to try and worm their way out of their predicament. "Aw is tha wha eh was, comfortin ye. De ye noh think he'd be better off comfortin he's wife, my bleedin mother, de ye. Or does her feelins noh come inte this in any shape or form. Or maybe yis id both prefer eh if I went back oua de room would ye?" Puddles father "Jemmy" who went by the nickname "Lakes" tried his best to keep a handle on the proceedings by saying "Listen Puddles, there's no need to be flying offa the handle so quick. Wha Rosey meant was ders nuthin goin on that meets the eye. Yur addin two an two an gehhin twelve, ye take after yer mother like tha. Jazes if I was te tell ye the amount eh times I had te pull her up over things like tha I'd be here te temorreh so I wud." Puddles could sense his father trying to muddy the water to his own advantage, it was a favourite ploy of his whenever he was dealt a losing hand. Exasperated, Puddles spat out "Do you fuckin pair take me for an eejeh or wha. An there's another thing wha der fuck are yeh doin here in my house at this hour eh de morning, ye weren't here half an hour ago when I was takin Josephine te school." This was Rosey's cue to step in once more, which she duly did as she answered "Charlene (Puddles wife and Rosey's daughter) gave me eh key two days ago for whenever I wanted te come over ye know. Like when things get me down with "McGregor" gone an me on me own."

Perhaps now might be as good a time as any to bring the reader up to scratch as they say, get the lie of the land from a hilltop on a clear day. The McGregor in question was not "The Conor McGregor" but rather Rosey's pet Jack Russel, who previously answered to the name "Jasper" but when his vocabulary began to extend to include an over- abundance of growling, little choice remained but to honour Ireland's latest super-star. However, living up to the name was to prove the undoing of McGregor as dog owners from far and wide could not resist to test his mettle against their own mutts who they pitched into battle against him. Try as Rosey did to keep him indoors, he always managed to evade her watchful eye at some stage during the day or night. It was never proven who it was who brought about his demise, but one morning McGregor's lifeless carcass was discovered on waste ground with a bullet hole in the centre of his forehead.

McGregor was to be the second male to vacate Rosey's presence that year. The previous January her husband "Sam" had decided that the garden of Eden could do with watering instead of the bars and saloon's in his own locality. It has to be emphasised that for someone who was notoriously known for drinking himself to death, it sure took him an awful long time to prove successful. The one saving grace he left behind was his body organs (barring his liver) were in fine condition for transplanting as they'd been pickled in alcohol for so long they were practically in mint condition which was more than could be said for their owner.

Now far be it for me to speak ill of the dead but Sam's passing did tend to set a few tongues wagging. Rumours, secrets, innuendo's, lies and the whole kit and caboodle, you name it, his tongue had barely commenced to kiss the underside of the coffin lid when the whispering began. Sometimes the whisperings got it right and sometimes not. Sam's propensity for drink was due to his own shame at his wife's promiscuity and his failure to control her. And yet nobody could truly state that they fully understood Sam's predicament and what torment a person really is capable of inflicting upon themselves in their love for another. To put it in its proper context, the pain had yet to be created that Sam would refuse to undertake rather than wake up the next morning and find Rosey gone forever. No antidote exists to mend a broken heart.

Puddles wanted answers and he wanted them immediately "How long has this been goin on may I ask" he practically spat the words in his father's direction but he was staring at Rosey while his eyes narrowed in disgust. They both tried to answer in unison with his father saying rather timidly "Eh just eh few days that's all." But his words were diminished somewhat as Rosey also replied in unison "Eh bout two months I think." Lakes face cringed in embarrassment (what de fuck) he thought. Their pitiful plight brought a sneer in response from Puddles but at the same instance his mother's face sprang to his mind and what reaction all this was going to have on her health not to mention among her neighbours. Had a gunsmith had the good fortune to arrive on the scene at that particular moment he might well have made a decent cash sale for himself. Puddles was in no doubt that with the proper equipment in his hands he would gladly have blown Adam and Eve to kingdom come. Lakes would have settled for merely placing the gun in

Rosey's mouth and blowing her head off, thus preventing her from saying anything more incriminating on the subject of their sinful ways. However, Rosey bore no such evil thoughts and just wished Puddles would fuck off and mind his own business.

What Puddles was really on the lookout for was some sign of remorse from the pair of them, Oh, hang on till I look over the folly of my sins and fill a bucket or two of regrets and lends a hammer so I can nail myself to the nearest cross. What Puddles failed to remember was you don't always get what you want in this life.

The next to throw their sixpence into the mix was the clueless Rosey, one of life's unfortunates who missed out the whole of her schooling when common sense was up for grabs and settled instead for helping her mother with her seven off-springs at home. Illiteracy ran through the family like diarrhoea but for some obscure reason all ten of the family exhibited remarkable skills at subtractions and multiplications. In spite of the hardships of their family background not one of them ever resorted to crime and all grew up to have families of their own with similar traits.

Puddles could stand it no longer as he stared his father right between the eyes and demanded "Did ye ever give eh thought wha ye were doin te Ma with yer carry on. How did ye think she was goin te feel when she found out, wha, did ye" Sheepishly, Lakes lowered his eyes to the floor as he replied half whispering "Well me an yer Ma haven't exactly been gehhin on these past few months ye know" "No, I didn't know," Puddles answered sarcastically, not for one moment believing a word his father said. Lakes, taking his cue for an opportunity to basically shift the blame unto someone else said in a defensive manner "Yeh yer Ma was always complainin about herself." Puddles immediately took his mother's honour a notch higher, as through clenched teeth he enquired "Wha de ye mean, complainin?" Once again the door was left open for Rosey as she interjected rather off-handily "Aw ye know, she was havin woman's trouble down dere" as she cast her eyes down in the direction of the floor. Now rounding fully towards her, with his teeth clearly showing against his lips Puddles demanded of her "An how may I ask are you so well up on my mother's condition if it's noh too much trouble to ask?" Without stopping to blink she calmly nodded to Lakes and remarked "He told me."

It was as if a knife had been thrust into his heart when Puddles heard these few words. Nothing but betrayal on his father's part screamed out at him. But then it dawned on him that there was also the betrayal of Rosey to consider. Meanwhile Lakes too was having thoughts of his own regarding being sent down the river in a one- man canoe with the boatwoman waving to him from the shore holding on tightly to the paddle. (I fucking told her that in confidence and now she's after telling him. Talk about shit for brains.) While Puddles stood there, all he could do was shake his head in bewilderment. Never again would he ever have anything to do with his father when all this was over, if ever. (How in the name eh jazzes am I ever goin te live this down. What am I goin te tell Charlene) Throughout all of this everybody was still in the same position as when the confrontation first started. Puddles was facing his father with Rosey in the background behind him. And strange as it may seem nobody had moved an inch either forwards or backwards. It was though the three of them had been caught in a time-warp and couldn't move.

It's practically inconceivable that anyone would attempt what Rosey done next? With tension already building at a steady pace now would not be an ideal moment to check up on your bucket list of things to do to help out your nearest and dearest who's being confronted by his demented son on the subject of his adultery. The thing is although they may have only been in cahoots with each other for the last two months, their friendship did stretch back for several years due to their off-springs marrying each other and rearing a family. Rosey liked to keep abreast of whatever may become available in the future and "Jemmy" was one she'd earmarked for possibilities. Compare it if you will to a butcher hanging a carcass of meat in a deep freezer while times were plenty which incidentally coincided with how she liked her men, hanging long.

Although it may have seemed a long time to an outsider, Rosey always relished the waiting period. To all intents and purposes she resembled a professional angler who was quite content to sit by his rod and let nature take its course. No need to go jumping at every little bite that comes along. Wait for when the big one bites, then wham, that's when you take a firm hold and hang on for dear life. The same principle now applied to Lakes, now that she had him squirming on the end of her hook, he was now hers to reel in little by little. Having him close by it was now time to offer him some morsel of comfort just to kind of let him know there were two of them in this here jam. And if the posse was going to be repelled the two of them better stick together, all for one and one for all, if it was good enough for The Three Musketeers no sense in her and "Jemmy" deviating from the script.

And just how does one go about tightening the bond of friendship, why with a little bit of encouragement naturally? Since this was not the ideal time nor place to offer that incentive bodily, well secrecy wasn't too bad a substitute to have in reserve. Inching slowly forward, Rosey kept her right hand on the blind side of Puddles and gently making contact with " Lakes's" buttocks, she gave his left cheek the merest squeeze. Maybe the reader perhaps is under the impression this was a rather daring thing to do under the circumstances but it has to be said their plight at that particular point in time called out for such action. In broad daylight, when one analyses this gesture, rightly or wrongly, Rosey has to be congratulated wholeheartedly for her nerve and audacity. A, she squeezed his buttock in an act of defiance and fun to show that her and Lakes may appear to be guilty of a serious crime against God and man, but they could still laugh at their own predicament. And B, the gesture was also her way of letting her fellow adulterer know she had his back and also his arse, come what may. And without a shadow of a doubt it can be safely said, Lakes was sure glad she didn't have his front.

When he felt the gentle squeezing of his left buttock "Lakes" felt every drop of moisture instantly pass through every pore of his body. He immediately felt as though he was about to crumple to the ground in a heap. But just as the squeezing abruptly stopped, Lakes sense's heightened in anticipation for what he feared might follow. (What in de name eh jazzes is wrong wih tha woman) he thought (who de fuck in their right mind would do somethin stupeh like that)

Suffice to say Lakes failed to grasp the message and instead, placed his hand behind his back and stuck two fingers into the air in defiance at Rosey. But before she had a chance to answer she noticed Puddles lean over ever so slightly and look in her direction and say "Whats goin on with you two. De yeh think this is some kinda joke or wha" Before Rosey could make any reply, "Lakes" answered "No, nuthins goin on" and once again adopted the schoolboy being punished stance of bowing his head towards the floor in silence.

Just as "Puddle's" was about to admonish them further, the hall door could be clearly heard opening rather loudly and his wife "Charlene" shouting his name "Jimmy" "Jimmy". She burst through the kitchen door and though distressed and tears running down her cheeks, immediately pulled herself to a standstill when she seen the three of them gathered in the centre of the room looking perplexed at her condition. "Wha are you's all doin here, did yis already know what happened" as she looked at each of them in turn and a puzzled look coming over her. Puddles took her in his arms protectively and said in a commanding clear voice "Don't mind them dirt birds, I'll tell ye about them in eh mineh, wha's wrong" Not understanding a word of what he meant and panic returning to her voice, she gripped "Jimmy" tightly and unable to hold back the tears, she stammered "It's yer mother, she's after gehhin eh bang of eh van outside de post office, a woman ran in te tell me, buh when I goh there the amblance was pullin away. De woman sed eh doesn't look too good."

Charlene was a manageress of a hairdressers some four hundred yards from the local post-office and it was her conditions of employment to open the premises every morning, thus Jimmy's first task on arriving home from night shift from the bakery was to get their daughter ready and taken to school each day. It wasn't easy these days of high mortgages and everyone had to pull their weight accordingly.

"Lakes" began to fluster and become agitated as he quickly began to button up his jacket. Puddles wasted no time in putting him in his place as he waved his index finger in his face and declared "YOU, you go back home an stay there, de ye hear. An as for you (as he then turned his attention to Rosey) you just stay away from him, I'll sort you's out when dis is over don't you worry" Charlene looked from one to the other with a look of puzzlement about her and didn't know what to make of it all while her main concern was what was happening to her mother-in-law.

True to form, Rosey attempted to have the last word before Puddles and Charlene departed and also not wanting to let her daughter see she was as meek as Lakes interjected "I hope yer Ma is alright, tha its nuthin serious" Puddles stopped In his tracks instantly and looking back at Rosey, sneeringly replied "I tell ye something Rosey, ye have some neck so ye have. After all that's happened te say that" as he grabbed Charlene's arm and pulled her after him out the kitchen door.

Unfortunately for Puddles and Charlene they were too late getting to the hospital in time as Chrissy (Puddles mother) passed away on the journey having being given the last rites by the priest in the ambulance. The van that caused the fatal collision had earlier been hijacked while transporting spirits between warehouses and was being chased by armed police.

Meanwhile, left to themselves, Lakes and Rosey sat down to debate about where do they go from here and Lakes was under no illusion but that the sooner he got away from Rosey, the longer he'd live. Rosey too, figured she'd be better off checking out fresher pastures as she felt Lakes didn't put up enough of a fight to defend her honour in front of his son. One thing's for certain regarding Rosey's future, irrespective of how many more years she was to reside on this planet, as long as there was a hole near-by, she was sure to put her foot in it big time. Now there's an ideal match-up if there ever was one. How about she was to take a little vacation up to Alaska and have a search for the elusive Bigfoot.

Who Will Be Waiting For You?
By Nicholas Earley

It was mid-November and a heavy frost was expected later on. Although it was only nine thirty at night the housing estate was practically deserted of human traffic. Whatever transport was moving it certainly moved fast enough due to the empty roads. At the main shopping precinct two forlorn figures made their way by stopping at some of the shops to comment on what they displayed. They were both long time ex-members of the human race; having long ago given up on life to spend out the rest of their lives in pursuit of the charms of drugs. Both in their early forties, it's reasonable to state they'd been lucky to live this long with their addiction. Most of their fellow addicts they'd associated with had long passed on through either bad gear, bad choices or bad luck, either one will get you in the end.

"Cats and Dogs" were the names attributed to our two stoners by all who'd had any dealings with them over the years. A fitting description it has to be said for that's exactly how they behaved towards each other before the plunge of the needle brought some normality to their friendship. The only thing that kept the partnership intact was no-one else would trust them enough not to kill them in their sleep and make off with the stash. "Cats" (Ben) and "Dogs" (Peter) had been through more than enough life threatening experiences to turn any normal person off drugs for life but to both of them it was all par for the course. Besides, who was going to offer them any sympathy? Both of them were mere shells of the men their families had such high hopes for before succumbing to the temptation of drugs. The same families who years later had finally called enough to their thievery, incarcerations, lies and always expected to pick up the pieces, irrespective of the circumstances. Included among the injured were wives and children who were also unfortunate to have passed through their lives as they continued on their roads to hell.

As they were both engrossed in commenting on the special offers on display in a travel agents window, neither was aware of a black 4x4 pull up to the kerb beside them. Inside were three members of a drug gang that traded in a neighbouring estate. Presently they were on surveillance for volunteers in a personal project vital to their employer's enterprise. A recent shipment of drugs had arrived undiluted and therefore before distribution could commence the quality of the product had to be mixed and assessed. And what better way to facilitate their requirements than to test it out on an obliging customer. Pharmaceutical companies dare not bring a product to market without first complying with strict guidelines regarding the testing of same. But drug dealers ignored such timetables and tested at source. Besides, where the companies spent millions compensating volunteers, the dealers had no such overheads to worry about.

Then the manufacturers had a time frame to adhere to before declaring their product safe for humans. Once again the dealers bypassed such restrictions and got their experimental results within a day or possibly sooner if the product was contaminated. Volunteer didn't make it? Back to the source and adapt some more, another volunteer, here we go again. You win some you lose some, plenty more where they came from.

One of the occupants alights from the jeep and makes his way over to "Cats and Dogs" "How's eh goin lads anyone up for eh smack of free gear, what" as he waves his little sample bag in front of their eyes. Now the mere mention of free gear to any addict is Manna from heaven. It's like someone offering you the winning lottery ticket. "Cats and Dogs" didn't have to be asked a second time and both eagerly reached for the packet. Now it has to be said the lads were not unaware of what was going down. This by no means was their first encounter with a dealer offering free gear, except for up to now most of the time the gear was absolute crap, diluted to such an extent as to be practically worthless. So who was to say this was going to be any different. Taking the gear, they thanked their benefactor and made their way out of the precinct in the direction of the football pitches close by.

The jeep now followed them both at a safe distance to ascertain where they were shooting up and bedding down. It wouldn't do to lose track of them or who they may talk to.

Having made their way behind a large metal container which was used as a changing room by many of the junior soccer teams, Ben and Peter erected their makeshift sleeping quarters from the paraphernalia hidden close by. They both decided, from experiences with so called free samples before, to chuck the whole packet into one hit and to hell with the consequences.

After draining the last drop from the needle, Ben slowly lowered his head backwards and rested it on the air pillow underneath, turning his gaze towards Peter who was already gently slipping away, Ben's eyelids eased silently closed. In less than ten minutes the emissaries from the spirit world began to cradle the wounded spirits of Ben and Peter to their bosom and comfort them in their confusion and panic. These were known as the light people and among them were some family and friends of both of them who'd passed over previously. Just as some doctors and nurses were needed to bring people into the world so too was help required to return them to their ancestors. At long last both of them had finally left behind the pains and torments of earth in exchange for their rightful place in the afterlife.

The next morning the pushers returned for to confirm whether their generosity had been to the junkies benefit or not. Seeing two ambulances at the dressing room and several paramedics busy and also the presence of the police it was obvious another test would be required and more volunteers needed. The sad passing of "Cats and Dogs" caused no remorse for them, just another day in Sin City.

PM Spunk is known for, but not limited to being a poet. Also a published, award winning poet/writer/author & a stand up comic of an alternative nature. PM Spunk is a Visionary.

He is also a promoter and digital artist/ marketing wiz that also likes to take time out and mentor rookies of the arts by giving tips and advice due to the delight he has in seeing other people achieve success in life.

PM advocates for Mental Health as he has had to battle his demons over the years and still does suffer with crippling anxiety and also has his on again off again relationship with depression.

He is a regular on the Dublin open mic scene and performs at literary and arts nights throughout Ireland.

10 Cents
By PM Spunk

Buddhism, toffees and crisps. The Bloods and James Woods. Hanging out with my buds. Hoods up buttercup. From our drink we'd take a sup. Alcohol Free is my way to be. You can't see me. I'll sell out any arena like John Cena. The haters try to hand me a subpoena. I magically wave it away like Sabrina.

I'm simply the best, like Tina Turner. On Family and Friends I'd never do a burner. I am the reason a person gets a heart murmur. I am a forever learner. Shout out to an old teacher, Ms Verner. She has a sexy ass but she could have been sterner. On Shrove Tuesday, I'm no pancake burner. I am the man of every hour. The yearner of power. I never cower. If I lose, I'm never sour.

I hate to lose as it leaves a bruise on my ego. Wherever I go, he goes. Where we stop nobody knows. We keep each other on our toes. Sometimes people don't know, where he ends and I begin. But that's cool with me as long as we win. I have thick skin. After I speak you can't hear a pin drop. I am top of the mountain. The haters are bottom of a fountain, mounting each other.

I have 2 brothers. Anto and Stephen. 2 faced people would have ya heaving. On the daily, I am conceiving ideas and rhymes in my mind. You won't find a blemish. Every minute, every hour my brain will replenish, filling me up with bigger and better ideas. I don't need any beers to have a good time. I became the best, at the drop of a dime.

Beckoned
By PM Spunk

It's only just begun but deep down inside I know you're the one. It was clear from the start that we would never part, you are always and forever in my heart. You are my sun in the sky when all I see is rain. You are my love train and my love for you is insane. You and me, we will always go against the grain. When others go left we'll go right. You make me feel 10 foot in height. It was love at first sight.

You make me feel whole. You intertwine with my soul, sharing my love and light with you is my goal. What's mine is yours; you and me will endure the sands of time, we will grow old and withstand the climb. Our love doesn't cost a dime. You are my one and only life line.

There is no denying, that when I'm with you I hear wedding bells. I have never seen any other couple that gels, as much as the two of us. With you it is easy to discuss anything and everything. You are the Yang to my Zing. You have my heart on a string. You are the King of hearts to my Queen. You are my mister to my bean. Whenever I need you are always on the scene. I love you more than Celine Dion. I love it how you act on your feelings and go head to head with your demons.

I look forward to our wonderful future together. You make my worries as light as a feather regardless of weather. I love how we can blather on and on about pretty much anything and you're not all about looks and vanity.

You turn my insanity into sanity. We live in our own pretty weird reality. I honestly love how you think my profanity is a turn on, like Chaka Khan said; Ain't nobody loves me better! And hand on heart; no one has ever made me wetter.

Our eyes first locked in a bar. It was The Lumineers playing over the radio. The song was HO-HEY. You really made my day and night. Before you, my nights out were total shite.

I'm always here for you day or night. Even if we've had a fight. You are my great white knight. I love how you kiss and hug and squeeze me tight. You will be forever my Mr. Right.

I love you more with each passing second. When our eyes first met, a life with you beckoned.

Lighter than most
By PM Spunk

My circle of friends is lighter than most. I love a good oul Comedy Central Roast. I love eating slightly burned toast.

I am your host, PM Spunk. In 1912 the Titanic sunk. Slam Dunk the funk said 5. "IT'S ALIVE!" said Frankenstein. I am the equivalent of divine inspiration, I am a poetry sensation.

Squirting, in layman's terms, is female ejaculation. Capital punishment should be the answer to rape and molestation. If alcohol is consumed, it should be done so in moderation.

Jerry Lee Lewis married his 13 year old cousin. My rhymes are not a dime a dozen. My audiences are always buzzin'! They never zone out. The Beatles recorded 'Twist and Shout'

Haters are all mouth. Without a shadow of a doubt. I am the best in the world at what I do. Whenever I drink one too many brew I always run to the loo. For poetry I am a major coup.

One Flew Over the Cuckoo's Nest. Just call me Gillette, because I am the best you can get. I don't do Ket; because I want hugs not drugs.

Jugs is another word fo tits. I love orange juice with no bits. I eat Jacbos' Cream Crackers not Ritz. The shits is slang for diarrhoea. Shout-out to IKEA!

Nice to see ya, to see ya, Nice. Tommy Vercetti is the kingpin of Vice City. I am the one man poetry committee. I am very gritty and witty. Molly Ringwald was Pretty In Pink. I am the strongest Link; Good-bye.

Pen to Paper
By PM Spunk

When I put pen to paper the words just spew out, more so than if I were to open my mouth. You can count on two hands those words I would say, but when pen touches paper, I can't keep them at bay. I can write all day and never tire, if I had a deadline it would go down to the wire.

People may not admire what I say, but I'm going to write it anyway. Despite what those naysayers think, I know that I'm on the brink, of something great, I will keep faith and know that I will shut down their hate, and on that there is no debate.

The words will rotate in my mind and people will come to find that I am absolutely one of a kind. My words will let people rejuvenate, so much that they'll hallucinate. They'll take the bait, I'll reel them in as I speak honestly from within.

R. P. L.
By PM Spunk

Fourscore means 80. To poetry and spoken word I am no Johnny-come-lately. My words will be forever stately.

Lately been thinking bout you baby said Samantha Mumba. Hakuna Matata said Timon and Pumba. Roomba is a robotic vacuum cleaner. Weiner is slang for penis. Bow down to my poetry genius.

I like Pepsi Max. A slang word for toilet is jax. A slang word for underwear is cacks. Frankie says Relax. Bleeding Gums Murphy played the sax.

The Fax machine has been around since 1843. A Banshee is a messenger of death. I don't take kindly to any sort of threat. I'd never use meth. Water is wet. Serial Killers mostly start off by killing a pet. I'll never be in debt. I'd never be caught dead in fishnet clothes. People can't get close enough to step on my toes. Those who oppose, say Nay. Fuck the Police say N. W. A.

Gay means happy. Anxiety can cause me to be snappy. Dappy said the Biggest enemy I've got right now is the tax man. Shout out to all the sexy ladies in Japan. Fuck the Ku Klux Klan. You've got magic legs, Lieutenant Dan, said Forrest Gump. When people are annoyed they get the hump. I once found a lump, I thought it was cancer. Only Smarties have the answer. Hold me closer tiny dancer, said Elton John. Will McKenzie is a briefcase mong. Pong means smell, my initials are RPL.

That Girl
By PM Spunk

There she was just walking down the street. It looked like all she had eaten was defeat. There was more track marks on her body than meat. Somebody beat this girl black and blue. Nobody knows who this girl is, nor do they care.

This girl is too embarrassed to share her life's dealings She abuses drink and drugs to take away her feelings and pain.

If this chain of events resume, I foresee, Jane Doe written on her tombstone.

Raw Truth
By PM Spunk

Raw Truth is never popular. It may not win you many friends, but it will get you loyal ones that are there till the end.
I'd bend over backwards for a loved one and never think twice.
But if it comes to spiders and mice well I'm sorry there's no dice.

Yes Sir.
By PM Spunk

Yes sir I can boogie but I need a certain song, I can boogie, boogie boogie all night long!!!!!!

I've never taken a hit from a bong. If something is wrong, dial 999 or 112 and emergencies will shortly be with you.

Krusty the Clown is a Jew, regrets I've had a few… then again too few to mention… Spunk'n word poetry is my invention. Ejaculation relieves tension.

Trish Carolan - I have had travel articles, short stories and serious pieces published. Reading my own work in some of Dublin's Libraries has been a real pleasure. I have travelled the world alone and volunteered in ten countries. My ambition is to write for TV.

Sticks and stones may break my bones but fish will never hurt me

By Trish Carolan

Every bump and crevice in each cobblestone made an impact on my bum. Hanging on to the cross bar of my father's bike I suffered until we came to the gigantic wooden gates of the fish factory. The massive wrought iron fanlight overhanging the gold crest of the "Fish Emporium" excited me because this was where my father and his brothers had their huge fish tanks full of exotic fish which they sold to pet shops. My seven year old fingers were too small to latch the bike to the railings but Dad always let me try.

Up the rickety wooden stairs we went to the perch where my father and his brothers over saw the entire Emporium. Massive tanks filled with much more than just fish covered the huge expanse. Train size electric eels snaked along the sides of tanks seemingly staring out at me. Sea Urchins the size of the television in our living room bobbed around, black dots in an ocean.

"That Manta Ray is winking at me Dad," I said.

"Yes, I can see that," he answered, I knew he didn't mean it because he wasn't even standing near me and uncle Larry was talking to him.

"Look Dad she, the Ray, is changing colour she's turned blue, Dad quick look. " But it was too late, he didn't turn around in time.

The arched half windows which were set between the roof and the red bricked walls began to judder, then the ice cold water hoses jumped up and swirled around resembling charmed snakes.

"Dad" I shouted, "help the cobbles are moving. " I thought I was shouting but my Dad didn't turn, he seemed oblivious of everything.

My hair stood upright, a tornado swooped into the tank and swished out the blue Manta Ray.

"Call me Cobalt," she said in a low soft tone, like marshmallow.

The sweet soft tone of her voice hypnotised me into her engulfing wings.

"Don't be afraid Rex," she said. "The building might be falling but a fish would never hurt you. I am here to protect you. "

I thought I screamed for my dad but I could see him still talking to my uncle, no one else seemed to notice this small earthquake and a huge blue Manta Ray dragging me down deep into the underbelly of the factory.

"Relax little bike boy, we love to see you coming here and how excited you are by our home. We decided that before we were sold we would show you our life under water. What you see is only surface level, do you get it, my joke. "

I was only seven I didn't understand.

The water heated up, then each of my arms and legs fell down as if dropped from a height. "Now you're relaxed, trust me. " said Cobalt in a velvet tone that was irresistible.

My ears picked up the sound of whistling, a whistling cat fish that's impossible.

"I'm a talking blue Manta Ray and you think a whistling cat fish is impossible. Whiskers, come over here and whistle a tune for Rex. "

With bends and swishes the doll faced Cat Fish came over whistling "The Gypsy Rover" my father's tune and I felt sad. A big black stone appeared flanking our right side, I froze. The pillow like wing of Cobalt cuddled me "That is one of the oldest mammals in the world,"she said.

"Tara the Turtle, this turtle could tell you tales that would set your belly aching for months, especially ones about stupid humans. "

"She has a fear of humans because once when she was on the Parathion Islands in Malaysia she laid a nest of eggs deep in the sand, then with her little flappers she covered them. Knowing that humans would come and try to steal them she set a trap. The humans pulled up in the moonlight along the lapping shore and slipped out of their row boats like jelly falling from a plate. Up the sand they sneaked hunched over in their black wet suits, the only things to be seen were their headband lights. "

"Tara had been robbed of her eggs before, she was ready for them. She knew that she could not save her eggs alone so she had her friend the eagle fly in front of the moon just as the robbers were about to find her nest. In the silence of the night, with the moon having gone out the robbers were disconcerted and maybe a little bit afraid, as they were given to superstition. Garry the Gibbon who lived alone on the island had grown way beyond the size of a normal Gibbon and he hated humans. Giving him the chance to do what he loved, which was to frighten humans, he screeched to his highest pitch while jumping from his hammock. The moon stayed still in the darkness and their boat mysteriously suddenly started to float out to sea. The robbers ran terrified into the deep leaving their equipment behind. They had to swim a fair bit before they reached their boat because Garry has a far reaching push. "

Cobalt loosened her soft wings and let me float up through the hairy coral and dusky weed towards light.

"Want to go home" Rex Cobalt asked?

"I am having such a good time I forgot all about my Dad he must be very worried about me. "

"He might be, hop up on my back and I'll speed you back, hold on tight now. "

My father dried his eyes on his sleeve while he held me so closely I thought I would lose my breath. Uncle Larry shouted "Group hug. "

"We thought we'd lost you," he said again and again. "It seems there was a sink hole where you stood, I thought maybe some big fish had come and eaten you like Jonah. "

"Ah Dad, never worry, bricks and stones may break my bones but fish will never hurt me. "

Winters Day part 1
By Trish Carolan

(To be read with a slight southern American drawl)

It was one of those white blanket over the ground days, I could hear the rustle of the tiny birds up in the high leaves and below the tinkling of an ice cold stream. Picture postcard you might say, not for me I prefer the heat. I could see by his demeanour that he was tired the black stripe in the snow behind him telling where he'd been. And to think it was only one year ago that he and I were belting down the hills of Monte Carlo.
 We sped around those hills like teenagers on Speed, he shouted back to me "do you want me to go all the way"? Wow I screamed you haven't asked me that in a long time. I can't hear you he was saying. When the road turned to sand I knew what meant. Yes, go for it I said. Pelting up the deserted beach sand whisking up everywhere I covered my eyes with my scarf and started to sing "We're on the Road Again, oh my dear Mama left me when I was quite young oh when I was quite young oh when I was quite young. . . "
One week back and the letter from the hospital came, this is it Baby he said, it's over. It nearly broke the hearts of our six sons and two daughters when he said he wanted only me at his side in the end. Shook me to the core but a dying man's wish is a wish to be obeyed.
So here we are on a Winters Day. . . Sings: I don't care if it rains or freezes as I have my plastic Jesus sittin on the dashboard of my car. Got myself a sweet Madonna dressed in rhinestones sittin on a pedestal of Abalone Shell. Glows in the dark and I'm not scardy because I've got the Virgin Mary assuring me that he won't go to hell. . . . .
You ok I asked? Never better never better honey. Come here and let me help you, just put one arm at a time take it easy. The brim of that old hat is gettin thread bare. I said. That look of despair flashed across his face, lines narrower than a seamstress's thread fanned out at the edges of his eyes. You're still my sweet heart I said, a mixture of sadness and love darkened his brown eyes and that old feelin of being

embarrassed at how much love glowed from him came rushin back, I reddened like a kid at a prom.

You want me to rub your back? Not now thanks, I ll lie here a while in front of the fire. You always were an incurable romantic I said. Just look at us, two old fogies living in a log cabin surrounded by snow and pine trees. We might as well be in a John Wayne film. It's the only way to go he said.

I felt like sayin it better happen soon, I miss my washing machine, dishwasher and television ashamed I rushed outside to get more logs. I knew we weren't totally cut off. There were the neighbours up the road and I had my mobile and my charger. It's what he wants I kept tellin his family, our family and friends, what do you want me to do? I could understand their exasperation and secretly I hoped he'd get fed up and we would just get in the car and go home.

Looking across at this lover of mine, husband, father and friend he didn't look sick nor did he look older he just looked peaceful. Sixty one years old is really sixty one years young nowadays. I am like a detached person, detached from my own feelings, my head, my children (which has never ever happened before) but most of all I'm detached from my beloved. Because this is just too darn hard. I act as though I am attached to him, but my heart and mind are kept in my safety deposit box for fear of letting out that pain, hurt, bewilderment and pure unadulterated sadness that at this point would be so overwhelmin I could never ever come back from where I might have to go.

There was the added pain for me of my childrens' pain, their Daddy leaving them all alone to face life without him. Their Daddy who had looked after their welfare for all of their easy going lives, earned money, brought them, taught them and most of all loved them.

The day was sunny two months ago when we called around the eight of them, two coming from Idaho and one from New York. I really think they thought we had won the lotto. They arrived in dribs and draps to our pretty suburban house. Neighbours all excited as to why there was a family gatherin. I don't believe my husband ever thought for a minute how difficult it was for me to keep that secret. Watching my own children, my babies arrivin without their children as I had asked assuming that was because there was going to be a big party.

I did say he didn't look sick, but that's because I know he should look dying. Each bright shiny face dulled one by one as they met him. The vigour and energy being stolen by one person and then the next as the rooms became stiflin. How do you do it? How do you tell your eight children that their Daddy, who after all is only 61 years old, will not be here in a matter of months? Never to be seen again. Well this is how we did it.

We cut off all outside communication including the doorbell, gathered them all into our usually food filled happy dinin room and then I said while holdin his hand "you're Daddy is dyin he has only three to four months to live". There are no words to describe what I saw then. This is what I mean about being detached. I viewed through squinted tired eyes six male faces staring blankly and two female faces (which I hardly recognized) convulsed in dismay and anguish looking to me for denial.

Their Daddy stood there as though he were caught in headlights; two by two the boys fell back on to the couches silent. The girls put their arms around each other and sobbed. Nobody seemed to think either of us might need a hug, not at that moment anyway. Then my darling husband did something unexpected. He took from his pocket an A4 page and began to read his Will. I was flummoxed. He had not mentioned one word of this to me, not one single word. Contrary to what you might be expecting as a reader there were no surprises. After he had read it aloud he said I know your mother agrees with all of this so accept it.

Like a cannon havin being charged the entire eight of them jumped up and began to hug us both cryin and talkin and questionin. There was somethin of a Christmas feelin about whole thing. For the first time in weeks we were separated my beloved gone to one or two cryin children and me to the ones who wanted a conversation. But talkin wasn't to last. Sadness ruled the evening and I always prepared had a takeaway sent in I also put up gin, whiskey, vodka and beers for everyone. Forty hours later they began to come to terms with the news.

He moves under the Foxford blanket now slower, more ill at ease than usual. I see the lines deepening around his mouth, that mouth that had kissed and longed for me at different stages in our marriage. That mouth that whistled after me up and down streets when I was a young girl, me lookin back pretending not to be interested. What a man. Still a little bit of television would have gone down well just now. I suppose if I had tele I wouldn't be writing this.

There's no point in me written more because you already know the end. So I'll sign off now and let you know that I am only 61 years old. I will have to live a long time more I'm sure without him my beloved but hey, what a memory what a life and love. Bye for now.

These are letters from this woman, now a widow, there's one follow up letter so far.

Winters Day part 2
By Trish Carolan

(To be read with a slow slightly southern American accent)

Well here we are again on a winter's day, what can I say my beloved has gone. A whole year has passed I thought things would be different. I thought things would pick up and I'd do things like other people do. Go, maybe to the library and read books on grief and sadness or maybe watch television programs, different ones than I used to watch. But to tell you the truth my heart won't let me. It's stuck in some kind of a cement shell. I cannot get it to move I try to connect with my children and my grand children like I did before. My love for them has not changed but my ability to connect as a funny childlike kind of woman which I was before this is completely annihilated.

I suppose I am a very lucky woman to have come to sixty without having to worry about bein childish. My husband, he let me be as childish as I liked, not foolish things like costing money or nothin but abandonment recognition of fun and just pure devilment. That has completely gone out of me. If you could see me now I look like a deflated woman. Remember I said before I was disconnected now I am deflated as if someone let the air out of my body from my temples to my cheek bones to my chin all the way to my breasts to my loins everything just fell south, pure unadulterated grief.

I cannot explain when I see my son, one of them, he is so like his father. Everythin about him, the way he looks down sometimes and smiles and then he looks back from underneath his eyes. The way he looks at me concerned and considerate, anxious that I be ok, it breaks my heart. I know that sounds like a contradiction, I said a minute ago my heart was like cement but the breaking part is not like cement it's the loving part.

When the kids come we sit down and have dinner, everyone is afraid to mention him then one of the grand children will say something like "Grandad would have loved this". I would just burst into tears. Then their parents will say "you've upset your Nana now". That is an untruth it is a chance for me to actually be myself to cry openly. The children cry, the grand children cry we all miss him so much. What is amazin is that death is the most usual thing in the world. The most usual thing in the world is to have somebody die on you and cry over them. But to me it is like nobody has ever experienced what I am going through.

On a lighter note, let me tell you somethin about him. When we were young we did some mad things. We went one time to a Greek Island, hitched all our way through Europe, crossed the water in a rickety row boat to this Island. We stayed there for months, drinking ouzo, buyin and sellin tents trundling around in big open backed jeeps. We stood up and let the wind blow through both our hairs', his hair was as long as mine then we both loved that wild abandonment it was something we had in common.

I don't think my husband needed a different type of wild abandon, at least I never heard anythin bad about him. But I needed it. I needed a wild abandon that would let me get up on a horse and ride along the edge of a beach thrashing through the waves. Sprays of white foam splashing up to my knees, chances I might slip off, chances that the horse might jump over some surprise. I loved being manically terrified by things and he just laughed his heart sick. He would say "you are one crazy woman and that is why I love about you. "

So in our huge sheepskin jackets, and before that in our Afghan coats, embroidered, we cuddled up together in front of the waves and melted into one another. People tell me in your sixties and seventies you can do that with someone. It seems an awfully long way off to me. I can't see myself ever wantin someone else. Maybe I'm wrong, even if I do take someone my heart, basically 80% will be left with my dead husband not with this new man.

One year, how can people expect me to think of a new man in twelve short months. It is not for me to be like that not for me at all, I adored him I lived for him and he for me and our family. I know how lucky we've been, but to walk up those steps across that wooden porch put my key in the door night after night after night after night is harrowin.

I don't go out at night no more I prefer to stay in, that way I won't get disappointed. I won't get hurt I won't have to face coming back to a dark cold house, or a bright warm lifeless house, looking at the things I left on the table that morning, unmoved, listenin for him, lookin to see his glasses and his newspaper just lying on the dinin room table. That's not goin to happen now is it?

I have no idea of another persons' grief but I know one thing, this is all consuming engulfing unadulterated pain. The cocoon of silence of relentless trying of wanting so much to break lose to get free for one fucking minute binds me. Just to be able to say I feel normal, just for one minute. It is impossible at this point in time. It is impossible for me. Other people say they feel dead peoples' presence beside them or they know they are everywhere. I do not experience any of that I experience, loneliness, isolation, misunderstandin, not being heard and disconnectedness. I have difficulty doing ordinary things that were nothing to me all of my life they now are just plain difficult.

Getting dressed, going out, being self conscious. I don't think I ever felt self conscious before. When anything happened to me I thought, in the big scheme of my life this means nothin to me because I have my beloved to come home to. Now there is no big scheme, my children have their own schemes my friends have their own lives. I am here lonely and said, I am sorry I will come back to you, I will come back to you.

Sings: Lover man oh where can you be?

I'm going to pack my blue up take care of myself, weep no more weep no more. . . . . . .

A Johnny and Joey Conversation
By Patricia Kane

From their high stools at the counter of the lounge bar two auld fellas, pints in hand, one with his eyes on the telly and the other one eyeing the growing crowd in the back lounge behind them.

Johnny: Well, well, hey Joey look who's sitting over in the corner.

Joey: I can barely see you, for god sake, Johnny. Who is it?

Johnny: If ya stop watching the feckin ponies for two seconds..

Joey: One of these days Johnny my horse is gonna romp home. Then you'll all be sorry ya ever doubted me horse sense.

Johnny: Shut up and look ya eejit. See your one sitting over there. Well my mother always said that your ones ma was a witch.

Joey: A bitch?

Johnny: A WITCH. Ya know, one of those scary auld ones who throw evil looks and spells at anyone who's annoying them.

Joey: Seriously Johnny? Did your mam ever see her spellin anyone?

Johnny: She told me that one night me da got fed up with that witch spellin everyone on our road and he was goin over there to sort her out. He had another large bottle to protect himself he said, from any scary stuff she might try to fling at him. Me ma said he then ninja weaved his way across the road to her house.

Joey: Jaysus Johnny, what happened?

Johnny: He never came back home ever again. And your one disappeared off the road that same night, leaving her young one to fend for herself.

Joey: Ah Johnny, what did your ma say?

Johnny: She said that the wicked witch must have thrown a spell at the da and turned him into something that couldn't walk home. She said that there was an odd looking horse on the green for a couple of days afterwards. And she thought that if the witch had turned me da into a horse then she'd get some holy water off the priest to change him back. But the holy water only annoyed the horse and it reared up and ran off.

Me ma made us pray really hard for the horse to come back but it never did.

Joey: Your ma could have been on to something Johnny. I swear some of the horses I put me few bob on run like old men.

Both laughed. The customers of the lounge fell silent at the pair's laughter. The barman told them to keep it down.

The Boy, the Bull and the Tale
By Patricia Kane

Long time ago, when stories and tales were not written down but passed on from person to person, there was a boy who being older than seven years was sent away from home to begin his apprenticeship in herding. His father was the Chief Herder of the Great Conchobor's magnificent herd. From as far back as he could remember he was always told, 'one day you too will be a great herder like your father'.

He began working in the fields of Cooley with the herd that had been sired by the great Brown Bull of Cooley. The bull was renown throughout the lands of Ireland and while the boy knew he was too young to take care of, or control the bull, he couldn't help sitting and watching the great animal when his work for the day was done. Oddly for a lot of those sittings he thought that the great bull was watching him. One day he decided to change where he sat to see if the bull moved as well. In the corner of the field was a stone, big enough for a boy to sit on but not big enough to block a great bull's way. So he straddled it, one foot in the shadow of the hedge and the other in the light of the field.

Not long after he'd settled the bull moved towards him. He came up close, blew hot air out of his nose and sat alongside the boy's foot in the light. The boy didn't move. When the bull had come to rest, the remainder of the herd followed and formed, for want of a better word, a cow fence around the two. Nobody outside of the field could see the boy or the bull.

The bull didn't make an animal sound when it opened its mouth, but spoke in the same language as the boy. The boy didn't move a muscle. His father had warned him of beings and creatures from the edge of their world who could bring harm or good fortune to a man. The boy waited.

"You are a wise and brave son of the Great Herder of Conchobor's animals, by staying still and silent," the bull began. "I have chosen well.

You will herd animals no longer, for I place on your shoulders the duty of telling my tale to all the clans of Ireland."

The bull paused long enough for the boy to rush the words out of his mouth, loudly

"My duty is to my father..."

But the bull seemed to ignore the outburst, placed a hoof lightly on the boy's knee and quietness fell between them.

"The Shadowy One has loosened her black flocks and they darken the skies of Erin more and more. Soon the sun will not be seen or felt. Trouble is coming from the land of Connacht to these fields and I am the prize to the victorious. Rest easy little one" the bull interrupted his tale as the boy tried to inch his way out from under the hoof.

"Your duty is not to fight or defend me. I know that Cuchulain and the boy warriors of Conchobor will fulfil their destiny and fight for me."

The boy waited for the bull to say that they would defeat the trouble coming their way, but he didn't. He simply went on with his tale

"Long before you were born, I was a Pig keeper for the King of the Sídh of Munster and I was known by the name Bristle. I had a great friend who was the Pig keeper for the King of the Sídh of Connacht and he was known by the name Grunt. Both kings were pleased with our herding. I'd take the pigs to Connacht and my friend would help fatten them. When I brought them home the king and his people would cheer and praise me for bring such fine beasts to the tables of the land. Then my friend would bring his herd to Munster, I'd help fatten them and when he returned home his king and all of his people would cheer and praise him as well. Our friendship was good. Until one day the Shadowy One freed hoards of evil doubt droppings and our friendship suffered. These evil doubts made people whisper in our ears "Which one of you is the best Pig keeper?" or "Which one of you is more powerful?"

"Being of the mystical lands of Erin we were both taught in the ancient ways and had the power to cast spells and change shape into many different forms. Our fighting began with the casting of spells on each other's herds. We caused the pigs to grow thin even though they ate and ate all that was given to them. Then our kings grew tired of our bickering, dismissed us from their realms, and our friendship grew more poisonous."

"We began to attack each other in different forms and appearances. For the first three years we fought as birds of prey, tearing at each other as we screeched endlessly. But when our terrible cries disturbed some of the great warriors of Ireland and they set out to try stop us. Then we changed into creatures of the water and took to the deep fast flowing rivers of Erin. The next three years were spent trying to throw each other out of the water or trick one another into the net traps of humans. Three years later we took the shape of magnificent stags that constantly clashed antlers. However we made too much noise and gave away the hiding place of the herd causing great hunters to attack. We took the shape of warriors and then phantoms and spent that three years fighting and frightening each other. Three years in the form of fire breathing dragons wasn't our best spell, neither of us could sit after our fire battles. So we took to the water again, this time as water maggots. In this shape I took to the rivers of Cooley and was swallowed by a cow, which strangely gave birth to me, The Brown Bull of Cooley. My old friend took to the rivers of Connacht and he too was swallowed by a cow that also gave birth to a bull, The White Headed Bull of Ailill, King of Connacht."

The bull was quiet and the boy pushed himself to asked,

"If you are here in Cooley and your friend is in Connacht, how can there be trouble between you?"

A large black flock passed slowly overhead and the bull stood up.

"The trouble comes in the shape of Ailill's Queen, who will not rest until she has both bulls or nobody has a bull. Cuchulain has taken himself to the border, I must prepare for our next battle and it will be our last. You must stay with the herd; they will protect and keep you from harm until such a time that it is safe for you to retell my tale. Tell it well, tell it straight and tell it true."

And with that the Brown Bull of Cooley walked through the herd and didn't look back. The herd closed and the boy didn't move.

The Handshake
By Patricia Kane

The whispers of the grieving congregation were not all about the dear departed. For those who lived and shared the past with the deceased, their whispers were of whether or not he, the ex-husband would show his face?

Their curiosity was satisfied when, as the priest came onto the altar to begin the ceremony, the double doors at the back of the church opened. Every head turned. Chris couldn't help enjoying his grand entrance. It would give the town's busy bodies fodder for a long time to come. His show of bravado weaken when his eyes locked on the lone coffin in front of the altar. If somebody had tried to convince him that a lifetime of memories could flood a mind in a brief moment, he would have dismissed them as spoofers or drunken idiots or both.

She had been the biggest prize in the town in those days. Her pick of any fella who tipped his hat her way. He remembered the power of his want for her. He also remembered that his want was simply because every man wanted her and none had managed to snare her.

He remembered the feel of her small soft hand in his when he was introduced to her and his matter a fact attitude about the introduction. He knew that given the amount of attention she received from other men, his off handedness would catch her interest.

The sweetness of making her his own lasted until the end of their first year of marriage.

He should never have done that to her, made her a challenge, but as someone had recently pointed out to him that he had eventually set her free. Free to find a love she deserved.

He let the double doors close softly and walked quietly towards the man who had made her happy. He knew that every eye in the church was on him as he walked towards the front pew. He placed his hand on her coffin then turned and offered his right hand to her grieving husband.

His hand hung in the air. Chris could feel the intense silence of the packed church.

Unbeknown to those present, he had made a point of seeking out her grieving husband the night before in private. And after a surprisingly comfortable meeting they both agreed that the woman they'd both married would love an unforgettable funeral.

So, they'd come up with the grand entrance and the pausing of the shaking hands.

Chris waited.

Bar Stool Preacher
By Peter Curran

I am the bar stool preacher
No pub in the land is complete without my tuppence worth.
On my perch, ready to swoop at any time.
Whether it's the North, foreigners, queers, feminists, Brexit or Trump
You ain't gonna like or lump my views.
You could say I'm an ugly creature
But you'll soon realise, that my views are right
And yours are shi....Not quite falling in with me.
Even if you are right and reasoned
I will subjugate you to the point
That the argument pool you jumped in
with me all of a sudden is about to deepen.
Oh please! Just stop your screeching!
About liberalism, equality and rights.
I'll always shout louder than you.
Even when you walk away from me.
You'll still hear me booming about the sissy views you're keeping.
I am the bar stool preacher
Reality is, I don't have any mates, no one will sit at the bar near me.
The bar staff hate me and ask me to get out
They call me the 'Tills grim reaper'
Because when I arrive, everyone is leaving.
I am lonely and all I really want is friends who love me.
To save me from a nights unsleeping.
I'm the one who needs teaching
In school I was the one who stood away from the group
....And was constantly ridiculed
In my angst and rage I sit here with my best friend Stella
She gives me the courage to tell the world who I am
A combination of an unhappy childhood and her
Makes me the man, whom no one gives a damn.

Governance
By Peter Curran

Sparks rise up to starry sky
Like rebels rise against their oppressors
A victory dance above destructive flames
With true belief, that extinguishes rapidly
As freedom soars through the heavens.
Years fly by, freedom is ruled by zealots
That beats, oppresses, subjugates its children
Societal outcasts are made by freedom
Single mothers, unloved youth, no future for them
New freedom doesn't want them to exist
"It's not the holy father's way"
The God squad shriek.
Like a brother's nails
Screeching down a blackboard
He laughs because it hurts the pupils ears.
Now, we politely sweep the past
Under an ever mounting carpet
That hides the shameful excrement
The innocents cry, no one really listens
The guilty stand like nothing has happened
Knowing authority and media
Will always protect them.
And we can still appreciate
The legacy our heroic ancestors gave us
And how we can still love the lord.

Family Tree
By Peter Curran

When I am dead and buried.
Please don't mourn for me.
On my grave, plant an acorn.
In the hope of what's to be.

In years to come, I'll shelter you.
Like when I held you in my arms.
When you were my little sweetheart.
Snuggled up so safe from harm.

When life gets you down.
You can come and talk to me.
Our path through life isn't easy.
Your problems shared under my leaves.

Each winter, as the snow drifts across my trunk.
You can keep me company.
For an Irish winter is depressingly long.
It will lift you up if you tend to me.

Let's chat about the old times.
Of who we used to be.
Bring your kids and grandchildren.
They can play in the shelter.
Of what's now part of me.

In springtime rejuvenation.
Have a picnic 'neath my leafy bay.
Share the stories of the good times.
Old and new, here the memories will stay.
In summers floral explosion.

You can play so merrily.
Kick around a football with your kids.
Like you used to do with me.

In Autumnal retirement
You can sit and reminisce.
How you've ended up so much like me.
How your chicks have left the nest.
Their youthful love you miss.

Finally in winters decline.
We can lay down together.
Again, at one we'll be.
Under the branches and buds
Of this our family tree.

Three Small Words
By Peter Curran

Three small words
So simple, so sweet
But do you really mean them
As you whisper them while we caress tonight?

Is it that you say them because you want reassurance
That you are unsure I feel for you?.
That I lust for your body
And feel nothing for your soul
Is it love you want from me?

Do you want to be adored
Like a wretched soul about to take my last sad breath
Seeing your light on the edge of the horizon
Like a beacon of salvation
Then forever be thankful that you pitied me

Do you want me to treat you like a god?
I'll be your lapdog
sucking up to your every whim
Your wish is my command.
I'll roll on my back, and you can tickle my tummy
Because that's what *you* want
Those three little words

They are only words, utterances, not true feelings
You don't have to tell someone you love them
You show it, like a young baby stares deep into her mothers eyes
From the very beginning
A union of love and adoration that most adults don't feel until they are
there, at that moment

Like the son holding the hands of his father
As he takes his last gasps of life
Saying so much in that final grasping squeeze
That Dad meant so much
As much as they argued, and hated

After this he will be so lost without Dad
Do you want me to say them flippantly
Three words; I love you
Or shall we slump in eternal embrace?

Spring Haiku
By Peter Curran

Winter chains warmed now
Beasts from east sailed away too
The saps are rising!
*

Daffodils tulips
Blossoms are all around us
Love is in the wind!
*

The sounds of birdsong
Migratory birds arrive
To our green pastures!
*

Everything to do
Now the days are much longer
Chance a barbie yet?
*

Men wear bright tshirts
People jog around the park
Summer is nearing!
*

So much cheerfulness
Winter is long forgotten
Everyone loves spring!

Winter Haiku
By Peter Curran

Frosty crisp underfoot
The snow is coming they say
When will it finish
Dark nights go on long
I hate rising in this dark
Summer sun has passed
Blue bottle buzzes
In hot kitchen, July heat
But not this cold night
Icicles drip down
Like cold tears from crying eyes
I miss the suns warmth
Grey slush on road side
Winters beauty is long gone
Splashing my sad soul
Full of emptiness
I wait keenly for summer
I exist in hope.

Winter Poem
By Peter Curran

Oh bitter December's winter morn
Why do you taunt me so?
So long, so dark, and miserable
When will springs warm winds blow?
A seductive teasing sunset dusk
A dim ray dances warmly on frosty nose
Then darkness falls, it snows again
Misery just never goes
Oh winter flowers you give me hope
To live at any cost
Snowdrops, cherry blossoms, mistletoe
When you show beautiful tones
Popping out in snowy frost
But woah is me, the darkness plagues
And sunlight is a lack
Oh when will I hear migratory birdsong
Of swallows, martins, swifts
Or feel the warm breeze and Jinny Joes
Brushing across my lips
I will just sit here in this void
Of a frigid Siberian freeze
That beats like a raw arctic cane
And smile in the face of adversity
Until a warm perspiring glow
Is beamed across my face again

Sinéad MacDevitt has been published in *Boyne Berries, Extended Wings, Revival Literary Journal, North West Words* and *The Reform Jewish Quarterly* and *The Flying Superhero Clothes Horse.* She was short-listed for the *Swords Heritage Festival* short story competition and highly commended for the *Jonathan Swift* prose competition. Her poems have been commended for the *Francis Ledwidge, LMFM* poetry and *Rush* Poetry competition. She was awarded second place for the *Desmond O'Grady* poetry competition. She was also a winner of the *Little Gems* poetry competition.

The Ghost of Diarmuid
By Sinéad MacDevitt

What keeps Diarmuid so present?
The shouts of O'Byrnes and O'Tooles:
muffled cries in Dublin's hills
or the command of de Barnewall
shielded by castle walls?

The RIC and farmer
who stir at dawn,
with the fall of the phantom fort
or just a clip-clip-clop.

Before one can ever answer,
the shape of a bailey is dusked
by abodes with drones of the rosary
beneath the star that pulses.

Lights streak the canvas of nightfall
as dew sprinkles California Hills park,
and wheels of *Johnston Mooney & O'Brien*
trundle towards Raheen Road's sign.

A cat climbs from roof to roof
that vibrate with *"Panorama's"* tune.
Heads poke out of windows
to watch the outside news

And follow lights that flicker
as far as Pembrokeshire
and follow a light unquenched
until it reaches Diarmuid's time.

John Finnan joined the Ballymun Library writers in 2016, to take what had been a vague life-long dream and turn it first into a hobby and then hopefully something more. He has written sporadically for many blogs and online journals over the last twenty years but never took it seriously until now. His background is in I.T. but as a career, it never brought the sort of pleasure that writing has brought him. He posts short pieces of work sporadically on his website : http://raymondfinn.wordpress.com

The Cry Of The Bean-Sídhe
By John Finnan

It's Halloween, the feast of Samhain. And not many outside the Emerald Isle know that Ireland is the source of this holiday. It has many similar relatives around the globe, such as the Mexican Day of the Dead.

A night when the veil between the living and the dead is parted, and the spirits and ghouls and ghosts and demons walk the Earth, while humans dress up to look like them. And as we all gather around the village bonfires, taking in the warmth to our cold bones, you could be standing beside one of the dead and not even know it.

It is a time for stories to be passed down - the True stories that teach us dark and sometimes terrible lessons, which could never be believed on any other night of the year.

True stories - like this one.

Hear me now.

My mother, may the light guide her and save her, is a god fearing woman. And while she would have lied to a child with all good nature and good intent, to play games and tricks and make believe, she would sooner dance on glass than lie as an adult. So this is as true a story as I tell you now.

It was the 1950's. Ireland was a relatively new country. The Emergency (World War II) was over, and rationing had ended. And the people were just starting to enjoy a little prosperity. Young women were entering the workforce, though feminism as a movement had yet to bloom. And modern thinking, modern science, had banished tradition and folk wisdom to the corners of Eireann's coasts where Gaelic was still spoken and belief in Faerie (the little people) was still entertained.

My mother was one such young woman, employed and enjoying the independence that a little money in her pocket could bring. It was now a possible treat for her and her friends to go out for a drink or go to a dance. And if it was all girls together at the end of the night, they could walk each other home, as her and her friends all lived in close proximity to each other.

This particular year, it was Halloween. A very different kind of Halloween than we celebrate today. In the countryside there would have been Harvest games and their own traditions. Leaving out saucers of milk for the little people. Or ancient traditions carried out at the local crossroads. Small packages of mysterious contents, prepared by the eldest grandmother and placed in the bed of the youngest child. But those stories are not this story.

In the city, there was nothing like this. So my mother and her friends walked home on the mostly empty streets in the chill October air, laughing and talking good naturedly. They had had a grand old night at the Metropole, having some drinks at first. And then later when the young men sauntered over from the Cosmo snooker club because their games had finished for the evening, a new set of games began as couples flirted and danced on the old wooden floors to the sound of the big band.

See it now, if you can. Under the pale moonlight, this group of five young women, girls even. My mother, my godmother Phyllis and three of their friends. Laughing and talking good naturedly, with not a care in the world. Until suddenly the conversation stops. Because there ahead of them on the previously empty street, as if by magic, appears a foul looking creature, firmly in their way and striding purposefully towards them.

This crone, and yes I use the word aptly with no insult, looked ancient. And not just in a way that all elderly folk appear to the judgemental eyes of youth that gaze upon their unimagined future. Ancient. If her skin was parchment, nothing more recent than Latin was inscribed there. And it would be a braver man than I, who would speak what was written there aloud. Her clothes were rags. In a way that would make a mockery of the truly poor. These were rags as imagined by someone who had never known poverty. Clean, but curiously patchwork, and resembling no clothing that was made or sold by human hands.

These oddities only stood out later, when the girls were talking about it amongst themselves. How the inherent "wrongness" in her clothes gave incentive to the stomach to turn, in the adrenal glands to run and in the subconscious to scream "Beware! Danger!"

But in the moment, there were two other things that stood out. Her eyes - fixated squarely on Phyllis, dark with menace and sinister intent. And most bizarrely of all, she was completely soaked from head to toe. From the long messy strands of uncombed hair that fell from her ancient scalp, to the barely concealed feet which were surely callused harder than any leather.

The evening had been dry, and the closest river was at least two miles away in the other direction. Yet this woman looked as though she had just been washed up on Night's Plutonian shore.

My mother and her friends stood stock still, unaccustomed to such a fright, but the safety of numbers and youth preventing a full blown panic or desertion of their friend. Phyllis for her part, was as helpless as a trapped deer under the eyes of a merciless predator.

She stalked right up to the young woman, and with one gnarled finger she pressed hard into her chest, and spoke "Give me a cigarette, for I am cold and wet. It will keep me warm."

None of the girls were smoking, though in truth they were all smokers, well on their way to developing the lifelong habit that would claim three of them in later life. Smoking was very common in those days. It was not particularly unusual that a stranger could assume a young woman was a smoker. But this stranger did not ask the group for a cigarette. Nor for any other charity. She was single mindedly asking Phyllis.

And Phyllis, may the light bless her spirit and give it rest, decided to say No.

Was it bravery? Was it foolishness? You can decide for yourselves what you might have done in her position. I know because I asked - it was neither. It was simply the fact that she had a brand new unopened packet and wanted them all for herself. Is that selfish? Perhaps. Perhaps not. It might be more accurate to simply say it was not charitable. And charity, as countless saucers left standing that night attested, can keep a vicious spirit tame.

"I don't have any," lied Phyllis making insincere but steady eye-contact with the half drowned hag.

The disgusting looking finger withdrew barely an inch, and stabbed forward again with impotent rage and fury, its caked fingernail digging into her chest like the talon of an angry bird.

"Liar!" she hissed.

And then to the indescribable relief of the young women, she walked around them and stalked off into the night, still inexplicably dripping wet. She never looked back to them, my mother swears she checked several times to see if they were being followed and they never were.

The rest of the journey to their respective houses was still unquiet, but now there was no giddy laughter. As they reached the homes of their friends, the group shrank until finally it was just Phyllis and my mother. They lived on opposite sides of a green field and could see each others doorways from their own. Both still lived with their parents, as was tradition in old Ireland until you got married.

Nevertheless, my mother asked her "Phyllis, are you sure you don't want to stop here for the night? Sam has gone off to England, so his room is free. Me mam won't mind and you can go home tomorrow after breakfast."

"Don't be silly Dinah," she was told. "Sure I'm only across the way and I'll sleep in me own bed." But she embraced her friend before leaving and whispered to her with all sincerity "Thank you for the offer."

My mother stayed in her doorway watching Phyllis walk across the field. It was the longest five minutes she could remember. And it was with profound relief she exhaled when she saw Phyllis open her hall door safely and step inside, closing the door quietly behind her.

The silence of the night closed in around Phyllis with the closing of the door. She hastened to her bed, eager to draw the veil of sleep between her and the night. And perhaps sleep came quickly. Perhaps she dreamed. Or perhaps this really happened...

Phyllis sat up with a start. Outside, as loud as you like, was a cry. A keen wailing cry, sobbing as only a human can. On and on, she keened, as the sound cut through the night air like a knife stabbing into her ear drums. Had the crazy witch followed her home? Phyllis wondered.

Certain that her neighbours must surely hear it, and content to let them deal with her, Phyllis turned and buried her head under her pillow. Only for the noise to get suddenly impossibly louder!

Phyllis quickly rose, convinced beyond all rational though that the noise was in her very room. How else could the walls themselves be vibrating with such parasitic harmonies? But she was alone, in the dark, with the cry and her own guilt.

Her hands darted for the pocket of her discarded coat and clenched the unopened pack of cigarettes. She stormed over to her bedroom window, flung it open and hurled the pack into the waiting starless void beyond shouting "Take your smokes then!!"

Like the flick of a switch the noise stopped. Phyllis got back into bed and remembered nothing else.

The next morning though as she left for work, she found the pack lying there on the bone dry path. The pack was soaked through. Utterly ruined.

Only one cigarette was missing.

The nth circle of hell
By John Finnan

And then Susan turned around and said "Still, it was a great day, wasn't it?"

The inside of the van was just bright enough to make out her smile. It was a little uneasy. Perhaps from the bruising she had recently taken.

"Who ever knew paintballing would be so..." she paused, looking for the right word.

"Painful!" shouted Dennis.

The six of them laughed. All piled into the back of a van, they were leaving Splatoon behind and going to a pub for some welcome drinks, but for now, they had to suffer the bends and potholes of Ireland's back roads, while the ancient suspension tenderised their existing bruises.

"I'm going to remember," said John, a little quietly.

"Which part?" asked Ingrid. "The way you took that hill? That was amazing!"

He looked up. "What? Oh. No. I was thinking of something else... Never mind. It's gone now."

More laughter. Memories have a tendency to dim. It's what they do.

There was a collective sigh. Good memories.

"Anyone got a joke?" asks Derek.

"Yeah, I got one," says Dennis.

"There's this pregnant woman, see. And she is caught in a bank robbery. And she is shot in the belly three times."

"Oh! That's terrible!" cried Susan.

"What?"

"That's terrible!" she repeated. "Where was this?"

"It's a fucking joke, Susan. Pay attention."

There was an outburst of laughter at this.

In the darkness, John looked at Dennis, telling the joke. He already knew it. It was the three bullets joke.

One of the things which John found annoying was when someone tried to tell a joke and made a mess of it.

He was willing Dennis not to mess this up.

"So the woman is pregnant, and shot, right? And she is taken to the hospital. And she's all like 'Is my baby going to be okay?' and that. But the doctors tell her the baby is going to be fine."

"And then right, years go by. And the doctor, I mean the daughter, I mean, the oldest daughter, well one day she comes in and she says- Oh wait, did I mention that she was having triplets?"

John bit the inside of his cheek. Listening to this was agony for him.

Five long minutes later, Dennis finally reaches the punch line, like a marathon runner. "No, I was having a wank and I shot the cat!"

Everyone erupted in laughter, except for John. And then a voice in the dark said "I'm fucking sick of that joke."

After a few minutes, Paulo asked "Any idea where we are, Derek?"

"Not a clue, man" was the reply. Derek stared out the window. "I just wish there was some fucking lights out there."

"Yeah, maybe the driver wouldn't have to hit every single fucking pothole."

"And maybe he could go a little faster than my fucking granny!"

"Is it even worthwhile stopping for a drink now?" asked Dennis to the group as a whole.

"Fuck yeah," said a voice from the back. "I can't be the only one dying for a pint."

"We should really do this again," said Ingrid. There was silence at that.

"I'm sure we will" said the voice from the back, dripping with sarcasm.

John said quietly "No. Surely everyone else knows this. We can talk about doing this again, but we won't. That's the way of things though, isn't it?"

Dennis added "Yeah. That photo they took of us all? As a group? We'll probably never even see that."

"Christ all-fucking mighty, that's morbid," said Paulo. "We won't be taking you two fucking bastards back anyway."

Again, there was a bit of laughter. Paulo could swear like no-one else, but he meant no harm by it.

"I can't help it," said John. "It's this fucking trip."

"Look at that!" cried Elaine. She was pressing her face up against the glass, staring out into the black beyond. The fact that there was no light in the back of the van, made it possible to make some detail out through the glass.

"What is it?" asked Susan, her sister, putting her face next to hers.

"It looks like a van. Going back to the paintballing place. Look, across the way there!"

Derek scoffed loudly. "What mad bastards would play a game like that in the dark?"

"I don't know. It could be fun, hunting down human prey in the dark. Use glow-in-the-dark-paint balls." Elaine did not seem to want to let go of the idea.

"Oh, give over Heffalump."

That other voice from the back of the van. People turned around, to look at the bald guy who had just committed the outrageous faux-pas of using Elaine's office nickname to her face.

"What did you call me?" she asked.

Aidan, they knew, was a friend of Johns.

"No one's going to be playing in the dark." He did not revisit the nickname. And the guys in the van, who used it often enough in the workplace, held their breath hoping Elaine would let it go.

She did. And there was an uneasy silence.

"We could be playing in the dark," said Susan. Once again, she wished to fill in the silence with something light hearted. "Roaming hands, no one to see…" She giggled a delightfully smutty girly laugh.

Elaine took up the laughter, putting her head on Susan's shoulder. "I guess if we were all travelling like this long enough, we would get to know each other intimately."

"Eventually."

"Maybe."

"Depends on what you mean by intimately,"

"PHWOOR!"

There was a chorus of good natured agreement and approval from the others.

Then Aidan said "It would take longer than forever for you to get a shag in this van, unless it was one of those sympathy shags from your sister." He laughed, and it sounded cruel.

"Aw man, would you ever shut up?" said Paulo.

"No" said Aidan conversationally. "Now don't get me wrong," and Paolo could suddenly make out in the dim light of Aidan's cigarette, that he was looking directly at him. "Truth is, Susan's arse is so fucking good, I'd consider shagging Elaine just to get close to it."

Paulo was shocked, not by the vulgarity of it, but by recognition. He had said that very same thing himself, and brought gales of laughter, over one lunchtime.

In shame, he turned aside. He thought to himself, "I'll fucking kill John. He must have told that bald headed bastard what I said."

"You've got some interesting friends, John" said Susan. She didn't sound pleased.

"Yeah, it's the quiet ones you've got to watch out for," said Ingrid. She tapped John on the arm, "Although I've got to say, when we get back to the office, I won't be calling you 'the quiet John' again."

"I thought Dennis was the quiet one," said John.

"You both are," laughed Ingrid. "But I won't say it again. You two were freaking dangerous out there!"

"Aye," said Dennis, feeling proud of himself. "I was pretty amazing, wasn't I?"

There was some laughter again.

"The quiet ones are always the dangerous ones," said Ingrid.

"What?" said Aidan. "Did you tell her about that girl you attacked?"

John turned on Aidan in an instant. "Fuck off, you foul mouthed bastard!"

"Ooooooo," said Aidan, "Handbags at dawn!" He made a sort of hissing noise with his lips. It was the universal signal, ever since schooldays, that someone had gone red with embarrassment. The sound was meant to simulate putting water on their hot skin.

"Don't worry John, no one can see you go red here. Blood doesn't show up in the dark, does it?"

Again, Susan tried to civilise the conversation. "I think I'm going to be red and blue. I was hit like, a hundred times! Once in my boob!"

"That was me," said Paulo with a grin.

"He made a habit of going for the soft spots," said John. "You hit me in the balls, remember?"

"Aye, I did," said Paulo, now with a wider grin.

Laughter again.

"Perhaps someone should have run over to kiss it better," joked Susan.

"With his luck, it would have been Dennis!" shouted Aidan. Then he laughed loudly, alone, sharing a private joke.

A few of them thought then, "I wish I'd shot you, you bastard." But none of them had.

Ingrid made up her mind to try and ignore him. She turned to Paulo, "A habit, eh? So was it you that shot me in the crotch, you swine?"

Her tone was easy and light.

"Actually no. Sorry Ingrid. That was me." Derek held up his hand sheepishly. "But it was an accident, I swear."

"Well all that red and green is still staining," she said. "I've a good mind to send you the bill."

Aidan again. "It wouldn't be the first red and green accident down there, now would it?"

"What?" Her plan to ignore him forgotten, Ingrid turned to the red dot of the cigarette in the dark.

"Well, maybe the little thing was trying to get home," he said. "Mommy, mommy!" he laughed, and then "But since you're from Drimnagh... MA! MA!"

"Fuck you," said Ingrid, now fully indignant. "I'm not ashamed of what I did. I had an abortion once. So what? It's not a fucking secret."

"Really? Well, that's great," said Aidan. "No, seriously, I'm a big believer in abortion."

For the first time, he didn't sound mocking or cruel, as he spoke.

"It's very hard for a single mother to get by these days. No one wants you, cause you're second hand goods. You can't get out on a Friday night, so it's not like you can meet a man. No man wants another man's kid anyway. They all just want to go out, date, drink, dance and shag." He turned his head slightly, to look at Derek. "Needing money, the mother is forced to work at whatever job she can get. It's either that or else she relies on Welfare. Or goes on the game. And in those circumstances, is it any wonder the kid grows up unbalanced? A social malcontent? Left to a life of school yard drugs and escalating crime until he OD's on some pills he's stolen from the local chemist?"

A chill ran down Derek's spine. He found himself thinking back to his own child. The one he walked out on, when he left his girlfriend. 'What was that now,' he wondered silently. 'Fifteen years ago?'

"Y'know," continued Aidan, "that's one thing I really hate. Pushers giving drugs to kids."

He turned his head now, and looked a Paulo.

"They're called 'loss-leaders'. You can learn about it in Economics, if you ever went to school. They're something you make a deliberate loss on, in order to secure an overall profit. Giving soft drugs to kids is one way to do this."

Paulo felt his stomach turn. He thought to himself "He knows. Somehow, he knows."

Paulo remembers that he used to be good at Economics, in school, before dropping out to smoke dope.

"Kids can't make informed choices or take justifiable risks," continued Aidan. "They are ignorant of the whole scene. Scum bags like those pushers should be given life. Or the bullet. Or worse."

For the first time, something that Aidan has said, meets with something like approval from everyone.

Everyone except Paulo.

The mood in the van was dark now. Collective guilt and shame stank the air, like sulphur.

Susan and Elaine, thinking of nights they had spent alone together. Dennis thinking of other times he had spent, with boys. Johns memories were filled with blood, in the dark. Ingrid was thinking of a child she never had, and Derek was thinking of a child he did. Paulo saw the faces of many kids, his customers, watching them grow old before their time.

Aidan stood apart from them, taking a long final pull on his cigarette, "Forget," he said, to the lot of them.

And in an instant, they did just that.

There was a long and uncomfortable silence, of the sort that happens sometimes between well meaning strangers. They were morose, but could not remember why.

Not one of them really knew each others secrets. So there was no group comfort there. No camaraderie. And Aidan would make sure that they didn't have time to know each other, intimately or otherwise, even though this was going to be a long long trip.

And then Susan, to combat the silence and make small talk, turned around and said "Still, it was a great day, wasn't it?"

The inside of the van was just bright enough to make out her smile. It was a little uneasy. Perhaps from the bruising she had recently taken.

"Who ever knew paintballing would be so..." she paused, looking for the right word.

"Painful!" shouted Dennis.

The six of them laughed. All piled into the back of a van, they were leaving Splatoon behind and going to a pub for some welcome drinks, but for now, they had to suffer the bends and potholes of Irelands back roads, while the ancient suspension tenderised their existing bruises.

"I'm going to remember," said John, a little quietly.

"Which part?" asked Ingrid. "The way you took that hill? That was amazing!"

He looked up. "What? Oh. No. I was thinking of something else... Never mind. It's gone now."

More laughter. Memories have a tendency to dim. It's what they do.

The TROCAIRE lesson
By John Finnan

School is a great place for lessons. Not just the boring book work, the rote memorisation of facts that provide the bedrock on which you can build the intellectual edifice of your choosing. It teaches other things too. How to make friends, how to lose them, how to fight and forgive, how to be sociable and how to survive when you're socially awkward. This was a different kind of lesson,

When I was a young lad, it was the yearly practice to give school kids a TROCAIRE box at the start of Lent. It might still be today, I don't know. Or maybe scandal after scandal or the rise of secularism has put our cardboard boxes Irish mercy to rest. But it was a yearly practice in my youth. And well do I remember the teacher in 5th class, Mr. Harkness, telling the class as if we'd never encountered charity before, how important our box was. How we were going to be giving up sweets and treats for Lent anyway, so we should fill that box with our pocket money, our allowance, that would surely be otherwise wasted on frivolities like having fun.

Now merely by way of background let me say I hated Mr. Harkness. That was a first for me. I was normally a swot, a teacher's pet, a straight A student. But not for this guy. I hated him. And truth be told, he hated me too. That was also a first for me. The origins of this hate/hate relationship are lost to memory, but given how well behaved I had been up until that point, I feel confident saying HE STARTED IT.

Also by way of explanation, we were poor. I don't say that to elicit sympathy. It was just a fact. I wasn't unhappy or anything. I just didn't get pocket money or sweets or frivolities. Lent didn't mean that much to me.

Now don't get me wrong, in previous years my TROCAIRE box went back after Easter filled with whatever coppers and five pence pieces I had managed to squirrel away. But I'd never felt shame because of it. Not until that year when Mr. Harkness made it seem so important to give so much.

I was a bright kid. I had faith in myself and I had no doubt I was going to succeed in life. So the idea came to me that I would, no doubt, in the future give money to charity. Maybe even a lot of money. I just didn't have the money now. So I wrote on a piece of paper "I.O.U. the sum of ten Irish pounds" folded it neatly and put it into the TROCAIRE box. Remember I wasn't doing this to be a smart arse. And I figured at least I wasn't handing up no box or an empty box. Even though you would NEVER break open the box to reveal its contents, a quick shake and you could no doubt hear the paper moving freely about inside. So up the box went, surrounded by other heavier boxes. Some ostentatiously sellotaped for extra support so full to bursting were they. And I returned to my seat feeling no shame at all.

That afternoon, after lunch break, he came to my desk and said "John, can I see you outside for a moment?" Of course he could. These were not actual requests one could refuse. I followed this wannabe mafioso out into the corridor. And he started his lecture.

I must admit, I rolled my eyes in that annoying way that eleven year old boys have. And naturally that ignited something in him, or stoked some fire already lit.

He was going on and on about the TROCAIRE boxes and how important they were. And my eyes were looking at him, but my mind was wandering and not really paying attention to him because that was the only passive resistance I could get away with.

And as his anger escalated, part of my brain had been listening, and told the rest of me "hold on - rewind that, that was important,"

He had just asked if I thought it was funny to write a note promising ten pounds.

Rather strangely, paying attention now, I could see something new in his eyes. Fear. And his angry speech rambled even quicker as if realised he'd made a mistake and was hoping I'd missed it, covering this misstep with hurried sentences that had no real heart in them any more. And then he finished with "Well?!?"

I hadn't really been listening, like I've said. So I didn't know what question he'd just asked. But I had been paying attention, to things other than his words.

And in my head, the thought kept bouncing back and forth across my skull. 'He didn't... He wouldn't.... He couldn't have... Did he? He **did**. How else would he know?

So I ignored his question, and in a voice steadier and braver than I can now believe, I asked one of my own.

"Did you open my fucking TROCAIRE box?"

I don't remember the punch of his fist. I do remember my head hitting the corridor wall.

It was the second mistake he'd made that day. I could see that in his face. As both sides of my head pounded, from the wall on one side and his fist on the other, I stared at him. This grown man, into whose care I was ostensibly placed for six hours a day. This grown man, who had lashed out in a moment of intense emotion.

As if the impact jarred the jigsaw pieces together in my brain, everything fell into place. He wouldn't have opened up just one box. He'd opened all of them. The way he placed so much importance on us all getting the most money into the boxes. He'd been planning this for a while. And it's ridiculous to think he was going to score big and live large off of the proceeds of this shameful crime. Yet he'd done it. Felt like he had to do it. And now his job was doubly in jeopardy. For theft. For assault. And oh the look on his face.

I don't know whether it was shock or some perversely smug satisfaction, but I didn't cry. I just opened the door to the classroom without bothering to ask for his permission and returned to my desk. He stayed in the hall. I'm sure he didn't know what was going to happen next. Truthfully, neither did I. He couldn't ask me to return to the corridor. But he didn't exactly feel like he could face me, I suppose. I'll never really know what was going through his mind. Because I never asked him. The fact is, I never spoke about the incident. Funnily enough neither did he.

I was haunted by the look on his face, you see. I learned an important lesson that day, and it's one I still think about years later. That teachers are only human. And some of them can be poor too. A single act doesn't define them. It doesn't define anyone.

I recognised the look on his face that day. Sure, there was fear. For his job perhaps. But there too, writ large as if in a mirror, I saw shame. And when I sat back at my desk and thought about it, for the first time, I really did understand TROCAIRE, which is the Irish word for mercy.

He was my teacher. And in his own way he did teach me. Maybe we even taught each other. I can't say. But I'd like to think so.

Acknowledgements
(Tanx)

I dedicate this work to my mother and father. To my lifelong friend Marcus Claffey. To my first and only fan Pilar Garcia. Thanks to Camillus John, without whom I probably wouldn't have continued this amazing creative process of writing. To Dylan Henvey, Helen, Nicky, Joe, Natasha, Kasey. Dermot, Patricia and Anne and the Ballyfermot writers group as a collective. Thanks to Cristina Revuelta. Big thanks to John Finnan for doing most of the work in getting this book off the ground. To Nancy and Trisha and the Ballymun writers group.

To the beautiful Paula McLoughlin for making the past year of my life bearable. And last but not least my daughter Violeta. Te quiero mucho de verdad.

Declan Geraghty
Aka "The Bowsie"